THE FLOWING QUEEN

Other books by Kai Meyer

The Stone Light

To Come:

The Glass Word

KAI MEYER

THE FLOWING QUEEN

Translated by Anthea Bell

EGMONT

EGMONT

We bring stories to life

First published in Great Britain 2005
This edition published 2006
by Egmont UK Limited
239 Kensington High Street, London W8 6SA

First published in Germany 2001
under the title *Die Fließende Königin*
by Loewe Verlag GmbH, Bindlach, Germany

ISBN 978 1 4052 2298 3
ISBN 1 4052 2298 0

1 3 5 7 9 10 8 6 4 2

A CIP catalogue record for this title is available from the British Library

Typeset by Avon DataSet Ltd, Bidford on Avon, Warwickshire B50 4JH
Printed and bound in Great Britain by the CPI Group

CONTENTS

MERMAIDS

The gondola carrying the two girls emerged from one of the side canals. It had to wait for the racing boats on the Canal Grande to pass, and even minutes later there were still so many punts and steamers milling about in confusion that the gondolier thought it better to wait.

'We can go on soon,' he called to the girls, keeping both hands firmly clasped around his oar. 'Not in any hurry, are you?'

'No,' said Merle, the elder of the two, although the fact was that she felt more excited than ever in her life before.

For days, no one in Venice had talked of anything but the regatta on the Canal Grande. Never before, the organisers announced, had the racing boats been drawn by so many mermaids at once.

Some folk slightingly referred to the mermaids as 'fish-wives', only one of the many demeaning names given to them, particularly after it had been claimed that they were in league with the Egyptians. Not that anyone seriously believed such nonsense; after all, the Pharaoh's armies themselves had driven countless mermaids out of the Mediterranean.

Today's regatta had ten boats on the starting line at the southern end of the Canal Grande, level with the Casa Stecchini, and each boat was drawn by ten mermaids.

Ten mermaids! It was unheard of; it broke all records. La Serenissima, the Most Serene, as the Venetians liked to call their city, had never seen anything like it.

The mermaids swam in fan-shaped formations, harnessed to the boats with long ropes that resisted even their needle-sharp teeth. Where there were footpaths people had gathered on both banks of the canal, and of course all the balconies and palazzo windows were full of spectators come to see the show.

But Merle's excitement had nothing to do with the regatta. She was excited for another reason and, she thought, a better one.

The gondolier waited another two or three minutes before steering his slender black craft out into the Canal Grande, moving straight across its breadth and into the mouth of a canal opposite. They were almost rammed by a boat carrying several rowdy spectators who had harnessed their own mermaids to its prow and, shouting raucously, were trying to keep up with the official competitors.

Merle pushed back her long, dark hair. The wind kept blowing strands into her eyes. She was fourteen years old, not tall, not short, but a little thin. So were almost all the children in the orphanage, except of course for fat Ruggero, but then Ruggero was sick – or so the orphanage staff said, anyway. If you slunk into the kitchen at night and gobbled up everyone's dessert, was that really a symptom of sickness?

Merle took a deep breath. The sight of the captive mermaids saddened her. Their bodies were human from the waist up, with smooth, pale skin that many fine ladies must surely beg for daily in their prayers. Their hair was long, for it was considered a disgrace among mermaids to cut it – and even their human masters respected that custom.

What made a mermaid different from an ordinary woman was first and foremost her mighty fish-tail. Seldom less than two metres long, it began at her hips. It was as flexible as a whiplash, as strong as a big cat, and as silver as the plate in the City Council's treasuries.

But the second great difference, the one that humans feared most, was the terrifying mouth that split a mermaid's face in two like a gaping wound. While the mermaids' other features were human and very beautiful – countless poems had been written to their eyes, and for the sake of those eyes not a few lovelorn youths had willingly gone to a watery grave – it was their mouths which convinced so many people that they were animals rather than humans. A mermaid's great maw stretched from ear to ear, and when she opened it her entire skull seemed to come apart. Her jaws contained several rows of sharp teeth, as thin and pointed as ivory nails. Those who claim that there can be no teeth more terrible than a shark's have never looked into the mouth of a mermaid.

Not much was really known about the mermaids. It was a fact that they avoided human beings, and many Venetians saw that as reason enough to hunt them down. Young men often amused themselves cornering inexperienced mermaids who had lost their way in the labyrinthine canals. If a mermaid happened to die during the chase it was a pity, of course, but no one accused her hunters of any crime.

More usually, however, mermaids were caught and imprisoned in basins in the Arsenal until there was some reason to fatten them up. Usually that was for the boat races, less often for fish soup – although the flavour of their long, scaly tails was legendary, said to be even better than such delicacies as the flesh of sirens and leviathans.

'I feel sorry for them,' said the girl sitting beside Merle in the gondola. She looked just as famished and even skinnier. Her blonde hair, so fair that it was almost white, flowed down her back. All Merle knew about her companion was that she too came from an orphanage, one in a different part of Venice. She was thirteen, she had said, a year younger than Merle. Her name was Junipa.

Junipa was blind.

'Sorry for the mermaids?' asked Merle.

The blind girl nodded. 'I could hear their voices just now.'

'But they weren't saying anything.'

'Yes, they were,' Junipa contradicted her. 'Underwater. They were singing all the time. I have very good hearing, you know. Blind people often do.'

Merle looked at Junipa in surprise, before remembering how rude it was to stare, whether or not the other girl could see her.

'Yes,' she said at last. 'I feel the same. They always seem rather . . . oh, I don't know, sort of melancholy. As if they'd lost something that meant a lot to them.'

'Their freedom?' suggested the gondolier, who had been listening to the girls.

'More than that,' replied Merle. She couldn't find the words to describe what she meant. 'The ability to feel happy, maybe?' That still wasn't quite right, but it came close.

She was sure the mermaids were as human as she was. They were more intelligent than many people she had known in the orphanage, and they had feelings too. They were *different*, yes, but that gave no one any right to keep them like animals, harness them to boats or hunt them through the lagoon for fun.

The way the Venetians treated them, she thought, was cruel and inhuman – exactly what people said about the mermaids themselves.

Sighing, Merle looked down at the water. The bows of the gondola cut through its emerald-green surface like a knife. The water in the narrow side canals was very calm; only the Canal Grande sometimes became choppy. But here, with the main traffic artery of Venice three or four bends behind them, peace and quiet reigned.

Without a sound, the gondola slipped under arched bridges. Some bore grinning stone gargoyles, with bushy weeds growing on their heads like shocks of green hair.

The facades of the buildings came right down to the water on both sides of the canal. They were all at least four storeys high. A few hundred years ago, when Venice was still a great mercantile power, cargoes used to be unloaded from the canals straight into the palaces of the rich merchant families, but today many of those old buildings stood empty, most of their windows were dark, and the wooden gates coming down to the surface of the water were crumbling, rotted by the damp – and not just since the Egyptian army closed in around the besieged city. The reborn Pharaoh and his Sphinx commanders couldn't be blamed for everything.

'Lions!' exclaimed Junipa suddenly.

Merle looked along the bank to the nearest bridge. She couldn't see a human soul, let alone any of the stone lions on which the City Guard rode. 'Where? I don't see them.'

'I can smell them,' Junipa insisted. Soundlessly, she sniffed the air, and out of the corner of her eye Merle saw the baffled gondolier behind them shaking his head.

She tried to imitate Junipa, but the gondola had glided almost fifty metres further on before Merle's own nostrils picked it up: the odour of damp stone, musty, a little mouldy, and strong enough to drown out even the breath of the sinking city.

'You're right.' It was undoubtedly the odour of the stone lions kept by the City Guard of Venice as their mounts and companions in battle.

At that very moment one of the mighty creatures appeared on a bridge in front of them. The animal was made of granite; granite lions were one of the most common breeds in the lagoon. Some of the others were stronger, but that made no real difference: if you fell into the clutches of a granite lion, you were as good as done for. The lions had been the emblem of the city down the ages, right back to the times when they all had wings and could soar through the air. Today only a few such winged beasts were left, a strictly regulated number of animals kept specially for the personal protection of the City Councillors. The breeders on Lion Island, up in the north of the lagoon, had bred the ability to fly out of all the rest, who were born with stunted wings, just pathetic little stumps on their backs. The men of the City Guard fastened their saddles to these vestigial wings.

The granite lion on the bridge was one of these ordinary stone beasts. Its rider wore the brightly coloured uniform of the Guard. A rifle was slung from a leather strap over his shoulder, dangling in an ostentatiously casual way as a sign of military pride. The soldiers had been unable to protect the city from the Egyptian Empire – it was the Flowing Queen who did that – but ever since a state of siege was declared over thirty years before, the Guard had won more and more power. Today they were outdone in arrogance only by their masters, the Councillors, who managed the affairs of the beleaguered city as they pleased. Perhaps the Councillors and their soldiers were trying to prove something to themselves – after all, everyone knew they were in no position to defend Venice in an emergency. But while the Flowing Queen kept enemies away from the lagoon they could enjoy feeling all-powerful.

The guardsman on the bridge looked down at the gondola with a grin, winked at Merle and spurred his lion on. Snorting, the creature made its way forward. Merle could hear the grating of its stone claws on the paved surface of the bridge only too clearly, and Junipa put her hands over her ears. The bridge shook and trembled beneath the paws of the great cat, and the echo of its passing was tossed back and forth between the tall facades like a bouncing ball. Even the still water rippled. The gondola rocked slightly.

The gondolier waited for the soldier to disappear into the tangle of alleyways, then spat into the water and muttered, 'The Traitor of Old fly away with you!' Merle looked round at him, but the man was staring fixedly over her head and down the canal. Slowly, he sent the gondola gliding on again.

'Do you know how much further it is?' Junipa asked Merle.

The gondolier answered for her. 'We're nearly there. Straight ahead and round that corner.' Then it struck him that 'straight ahead' would mean nothing to the blind girl, and he quickly added, 'Just a few more minutes, then we'll reach the Outcasts' Canal.'

It was cramped and it was dark – that was what struck Merle most.

The Outcasts' Canal was flanked by tall buildings, each as sombre as the next. They were almost all abandoned. Window frames gaped, black and empty, in the grey facades, many of the panes were broken, and wooden shutters hung askew on their hinges like wings on the skeletons of dead birds. The yowl of tomcats fighting came through a door that had been broken open; the sound was nothing unusual in a city full of legions of stray cats. Pigeons cooed on window sills, and the narrow, unfenced paths on both banks were covered with moss and bird droppings.

Only two inhabited buildings rose, clearly outlined, from the rows of crumbling walls. They stood exactly opposite each other, staring across the canal like two chess-players with furrowed faces and wrinkled brows. They were about a hundred metres from the mouth of the canal, and as far again from the dark cul-de-sac where it ended. Both houses had balconies; the balcony of the building on the left was made of stone; the building on the right had a balcony of ornate metalwork. Their balustrades almost touched, high above the water.

The canal itself was only some three paces wide. The water, which behind them was still bright green, looked darker and deeper here, and the space between the old buildings was so narrow that hardly any daylight fell on the surface of the canal. A couple of birds' feathers rocked lazily on the ripples stirred up by the gondola.

Merle had a vague idea of what awaited her. They had explained in the orphanage, telling her again and again how lucky she should think herself to be sent here as an apprentice. She would spend the next few years living on this canal, in this shaft of grey-green twilight.

The gondola was approaching the inhabited houses. Merle strained her ears, but all she could hear was the distant sound of confused voices. When she glanced at Junipa, however, she saw that every muscle in the blind girl's body was taut; she had closed her eyes and her lips were shaping silent words – perhaps the very words her keen ears had picked out of the jumble of noise. Like a carpet-maker with a sharp needle, skilfully picking a single thread out from a thousand others. Junipa was certainly an unusual girl.

The building on the left was the workshop of Umberto the famous weaver. It was considered sinful to wear the clothes he and his apprentices made: his reputation was too bad, his quarrel with the Church too well known. But those ladies who secretly ordered gowns and bodices from him swore by their magical effect. 'Umberto's dresses make you slim,' people said in the salons and alleyways of Venice. *Really* slim: when you wore them, you not only looked thinner, you genuinely were thinner, as if the master weaver's enchanted threads were consuming the fat of all who wore his clothes. The priests of the Venetian churches had more than once condemned the weaver's ungodly practices, in such loud and rancorous tones that the craft guilds ultimately expelled Umberto from their ranks.

But Umberto was not the only one to incur the wrath

of the guilds. The same had happened to the master of the house opposite. It too contained a workshop, and it too, in its own way, served the cause of beauty. But no clothes were made here, and the master of the workshop, the widely respected Arcimboldo, would no doubt have protested loudly had he been openly linked with his arch-enemy Umberto.

Arcimboldo's Divine Glass proclaimed gold lettering over the doorway, and there was a further notice beside it:

Magic mirrors
for stepmothers good and bad,
for witches fair and foul
and every kind of honest purpose

'We're there,' Merle told Junipa as her eyes scanned the words for the second time. 'Arcimboldo's Magic Mirror Workshop.'

'What does it look like?' asked Junipa.

Merle hesitated. It wasn't easy to describe her first impressions. The house was sombre, certainly, like the whole canal and its surroundings, but there was a tub of flowers beside the door, making a cheerful splash of colour in the grey twilight. Only at second glance did Merle realise that the flowers were made of glass.

'Well, better than the orphanage,' she said rather uncertainly.

The steps leading up from the water to the path along the bank were slippery. The gondolier helped them out. When he took the girls into his boat, he had been paid in advance, and he wished them good luck before gliding slowly away in the gondola.

They stood there, just below the notice advertising magic mirrors for sale to wicked stepmothers, each girl carrying a small bundle, feeling a little lost. Merle was not sure whether to take this as a good or a bad beginning to her apprenticeship. Very likely the truth lay somewhere in the middle.

Behind a window in the weaver's workshop opposite, a face flitted past, and then another. Curious apprentices taking a look at the new arrivals, Merle suspected. Probably hostile apprentices, if the rumours were to be believed.

It was no secret that Arcimboldo and Umberto had never liked each other, and even their expulsion from the craft guilds at the same time had not changed that. Each blamed the other. According to Arcimboldo, Umberto had asked,

'Why throw me out and not that crazy mirror-maker?' The weaver in his own turn claimed that on being expelled Arcimboldo had said, 'Very well, I'm going, but you'd be well advised to give that thread-cobbler short shrift too.' No one was perfectly sure about the truth of it. The one thing certain was that both men had been thrown out of the guilds for dabbling in forbidden magic.

A magician, reflected Merle with excitement, although she had thought of little else for days. *Arcimboldo is a real magician!*

The door of the mirror-maker's workshop opened, creaking, and a strange woman appeared on the path outside. Her long hair was pinned up in a knot. She wore leather trousers, setting off her slender legs to good advantage, and over them a white tunic shot through with silver threads – a fine garment which Merle would have expected to see in the weaver's workshop on the opposite bank, rather than in Arcimboldo's house.

The strangest thing of all, however, was the mask behind which the woman hid part of her face. The very last Carnival of Venice – once a world-famous festival – had been held almost four decades ago. That was in 1854, three years after Pharaoh Amenophis was awoken to new life in the stepped pyramid of Amun-Ka-Re. Today, in these times of war, hardship and siege, there was no call for carnival costumes.

Yet the woman wore a mask made of glazed paper and skilfully decorated, without doubt the work of some Venetian artist. It covered the lower half of her face up to her nose, and its surface was snow-white and shone like porcelain. The maker of the mask had painted a small, delicately curving mouth with dark red lips on it.

'Eft,' said the woman, and continued, with a very slight lisp, 'That's my name.'

'I'm Merle, and this is Junipa. We're the new apprentices.'

'Of course, who else?' Only Eft's eyes showed that she was smiling. Merle wondered whether some disease had perhaps disfigured the woman's face.

Eft let the girls in. Beyond the door lay a wide entrance hall such as you found in most of the city's houses. It was sparsely furnished, with plastered walls and no wallpaper – a precaution against the high water that often flooded Venice in winter. The Venetians lived on the first and second floors of their homes, leaving the ground floor bare and spartan.

'It's late,' said Eft, as if her glance had just fallen on

a clock, although Merle couldn't see one anywhere. 'Arcimboldo and the older apprentices are in the workshop at this time of day and mustn't be disturbed. You'll meet them tomorrow. I'll show you your room now.'

Merle could not help smiling. She had hoped that she and Junipa would share a room, and she could see that the blind girl was pleased too.

The masked woman led them up a wide, curving staircase. 'I'm the housekeeper here. I cook for you and wash your clothes. You two may be giving me a hand for the first few months. The Master often asks new arrivals to help – and you're the only girls in the house.'

The only girls? It hadn't occurred to Merle before that all the other apprentices might be boys. She felt particularly relieved to be starting her apprenticeship in Junipa's company.

The blind girl did not talk much, and Merle suspected that she hadn't had an easy life in her orphanage. Merle knew only too well how cruel children can be, especially to someone who seems vulnerable. Very probably Junipa's blindness had often tempted them to play tricks on her.

The girls followed Eft down a long corridor with innumerable mirrors hanging on the walls. Most of them reflected each other: mirrors within mirrors within mirrors. But Merle doubted whether these were Arcimboldo's famous magic mirrors, for she could see nothing unusual about them.

After Eft had told them a great deal about mealtimes, leisure time, and the rules of the house, Merle asked: 'Who actually buys Arcimboldo's magic mirrors?'

'You're inquisitive,' remarked Eft. It was hard to say whether she disapproved or not.

'Rich people?' Junipa put in. She stroked her smooth hair, lost in thought.

'Perhaps,' replied Eft. 'Who knows?' With this she dropped the subject, and the girls did not pursue it. They would have plenty of time to find out all that mattered about the workshop and its customers. Stepmothers good and bad, Merle repeated in her mind. Witches fair and foul. It sounded exciting.

The room that Eft showed them was not large. It had a musty smell but was pleasantly light, since it was on the third floor of the house. In Venice you never saw daylight, let alone sunlight, until you had climbed to the second floor of any building, and then only if you were lucky. The window of this room, however, looked out over a sea of red and yellow tiles. They would have a view of the starry sky by night and the sun by day – always supposing their work left Merle time to look at it.

The room was behind the workshop, and far down below the window Merle could see a little courtyard with a round cistern in it. All the buildings opposite seemed to be empty. At the beginning of the war with the Pharaonic Empire, many Venetians had left the city and fled to the mainland – which later proved to be a fatal mistake.

Eft left the girls on their own, saying she would bring them some supper in an hour's time – and then, she added, they had better go to sleep, so as to be well rested before their first day's work.

Junipa felt her way past the bedpost and sat down gently on the bed. Carefully, she stroked the blanket with both hands.

'Have you seen the blanket? So soft and fluffy!'

Merle sat down beside her. 'It must have been expensive,' she said thoughtfully. The blankets in the orphanage had been thin and scratchy, and in the beds themselves there were all kinds of bugs that bit you in your sleep.

'Looks as if we've struck lucky,' said Junipa.

'We haven't met Arcimboldo yet.'

Junipa raised an eyebrow. 'Anyone who takes a blind girl out of an orphanage to teach her a trade can't be bad.'

Merle was still suspicious. 'Arcimboldo is famous for taking orphans as his pupils. What parents would willingly send their children to learn a trade in a place called the Outcasts' Canal?'

'But I'm blind, Merle! I've been nothing but a nuisance all my life.'

'Is that what they told you in the Home?' Merle looked enquiringly at Junipa. Then she took the girl's slender white hand. 'Well, anyway, I'm glad you're here.'

Junipa smiled shyly. 'My parents abandoned me when I was a year old. They left a letter in my clothes saying they didn't want to rear a cripple.'

'That's horrible.'

'How did *you* come to be in a Home?'

Merle sighed. 'One of the orphanage staff once told me I was found drifting down the Canal Grande in a wicker basket.' She shrugged her shoulders. 'Sounds like a fairy tale, doesn't it?'

'A sad one.'

'I was only a few days old.'

'Who'd throw a baby into the canal?'

'And who'd abandon a child because she couldn't see?'

The two girls smiled at each other. Although the blank pupils of Junipa's eyes looked straight through her, Merle still felt that her glances were more than empty gestures. Junipa probably picked up more than most other people just by listening and touching.

'Your parents didn't want you to drown,' Junipa pointed out. 'Or they wouldn't have bothered to put you in a basket.'

Merle looked down at the floor. 'They put something else in the basket too. Would you like to –?' She stopped short.

'See it?' Junipa finished the sentence, with a grin.

'Sorry.'

'No need to be sorry. I can feel it instead. Do you have it with you?'

'Always, wherever I go. A girl in the orphanage once tried to steal it. I pulled almost all her hair out.' She laughed, rather ashamed of herself. 'Well, I was only eight at the time.'

Junipa laughed too. 'Then I'd better tie mine safely up at night.'

Merle gently touched Junipa's hair. It was thick, and as pale as a Snow Queen's tresses.

'Well?' asked Junipa. 'What else was in your wicker basket?'

Merle stood up, opened her bundle and took out her most precious possession – strictly speaking, her only possession, apart from the plain, much-mended dress that she had brought as a change of clothing.

It was a hand-mirror about the same size as her face, oval and with a short handle. The frame was made of a dark metal alloy that certain greedy eyes in the orphanage had taken for dull gold. But it wasn't gold, or any other metal that anyone had ever heard of, for it was diamond-hard.

The most unusual thing about the mirror, however, was its surface, which consisted not of glass but of water. You could dip your hand into it and make little waves, but whichever way you turned the mirror, not a single drop ever spilled out.

Merle placed the handle in Junipa's open hand, and the blind girl's fingers immediately closed round it. Instead of feeling the mirror, however, she held it up to her ear.

'It's whispering,' she said quietly.

Merle was surprised. 'Whispering? I've never heard anything in it.'

'No, but you're not blind.' A small vertical line had appeared between Junipa's brows. She was concentrating. 'There are several of them. I can't make out the words, there are too many voices and they're too far away. But they're whispering to each other.' Junipa lowered the mirror and ran her left hand round the oval frame. 'Is it a picture?' she asked.

'No, a mirror,' replied Merle. 'But – don't be scared – but it's made of water.'

Junipa showed no surprise, as if this were something perfectly natural. Only when she put out a fingertip and touched the surface of the water did she give a sudden start.

'It's cold,' she said.

Merle shook her head. 'No, it isn't. The water in the mirror is always warm. And you can dip things right into it, but when you take them out again, they're dry.'

Junipa touched the water again. 'It feels icy cold to me.'

Merle took the mirror from her hand and dipped her own forefinger and middle finger into it. 'It's warm,' she insisted, almost defiantly. 'It's never been cold, not as far back as I can remember.'

'Has anyone else ever touched it? Except for you, I mean.'

'Well, no, not till now. Once I was going to let a nun who came to see us in the orphanage touch the mirror, but she was terribly frightened and said it was the Devil's work.'

Junipa thought. 'Perhaps the water feels cold to everyone except its owner.'

Merle frowned. 'Could be.' She looked at the surface, which was still moving slightly. Her distorted, rippling reflection looked back at her.

'Are you planning to show it to Arcimboldo?' asked Junipa. 'After all, he knows about magic mirrors.'

'I don't think so. Not at once, anyway. Maybe later.'

'You're afraid he'll take it away from you.'

'Wouldn't you be?' Merle sighed. 'It's all that I have left of my parents.'

'*You* are a part of your parents, don't forget that.'

Merle said nothing for a moment. She was wondering whether she could trust Junipa. Should she tell the blind girl the whole truth? At last she looked at the door, to make sure no one could hear them, and whispered, 'The water isn't all.'

'What do you mean?'

'I can dip my whole arm into the mirror and it doesn't come out on the other side.' Indeed, the back of the mirror was made of the same hard metal as the frame.

'Can you do it now?' asked Junipa, amazed. 'I mean, this very moment?'

'If you like.' Merle let first her fingers slip into the water of the mirror, then her hand and finally her whole arm. It might have disappeared from the world entirely.

Junipa put out her hand and felt her way down from Merle's shoulder to the mirror frame. 'What does it feel like?'

'Very warm,' Merle told her. 'Comfortably warm, not too hot.' She lowered her voice. 'And sometimes I feel something else too.'

'What?'

'A hand.'

'A . . . hand?'

'Yes. It takes mine, very gently, and holds it.'

'It holds tight?'

'Not *tight*. Just . . . well, it just holds my hand. Like friends do. Or –'

'Or parents?' Junipa was looking at her intently. 'You think it's your mother or father in there, holding your hand?'

Merle didn't like to talk about it. All the same, she felt she could trust Junipa. After a brief hesitation, she overcame her shyness.

'Well, it's possible, isn't it? I mean, they were the ones who put the mirror in the basket with me. Maybe they did it to keep in touch with me somehow, so I'd know they were still there . . . somewhere.'

Junipa nodded slowly, but she didn't seem entirely

convinced. It was more of an understanding nod. A little sadly, she said, 'I imagined for ages that my father was a gondolier. I know the gondoliers are the most handsome men in Venice . . . I mean, everyone knows that, even though I can't see them.'

'They're not *all* handsome,' objected Merle.

Junipa's voice sounded dreamy. 'And I imagined my mother was a water-carrier from the mainland.'

The water-carriers who sold drinking water from great pitchers in the streets were certainly claimed to be the loveliest women far and wide and, as with the gondoliers, there was a grain of truth in these tales.

Junipa went on, 'So I imagined my parents being these two beautiful people, as if that would say something about me too. About my real self. I even tried making excuses for them. I told myself that two such perfect creatures couldn't be seen around with a sick child. I talked myself into thinking they had a right to abandon me.' Suddenly she shook her head so hard that her pale blonde hair flew wildly around it. 'But now I know all that's nonsense. Perhaps my parents are beautiful, perhaps they're ugly. Perhaps they're not even alive any more. But it's nothing to do with me, don't you see? I'm the person I am, that's what matters. And my parents were wrong just to throw a helpless child out into the streets.'

Merle felt very moved as she listened. She knew what Junipa meant, even if she couldn't see what it had to do with her and the hand in her mirror.

'You mustn't pretend to yourself, Merle,' said the blind girl. She sounded much wiser than her years. 'Your parents didn't want you. That's why they put you in the wicker basket. And if someone reaches out a hand to you in your mirror, it doesn't necessarily have to be your mother or your father. What you're feeling is some kind of magic, Merle. And you have to go very, very carefully with magic.'

For a brief moment Merle felt a surge of anger. She told herself indignantly that Junipa had no right to say such things, to rob her of her hopes, of all the dreams she'd had when that other person held her hand in the mirror. Then she realised that Junipa was only being honest, and to be honest is the best gift you can give someone at the beginning of a friendship.

Merle put the mirror under her pillow. She knew that it wouldn't break, and she knew that, however hard the fabric pressed down on the surface of the water, it would not get wet or soak up the liquid. Then she sat down beside Junipa again and put her arm round her. The blind girl returned her embrace, and so they held each other like sisters, like two people who had no secrets from each other. It was such an overwhelming sense of closeness and understanding that, for a while, it seemed even better than the gentle strength of the hand in the mirror that had won Merle's trust.

When the girls let go of each other, Merle said, 'You can try it if you like.'

'The mirror?' Junipa shook her head. 'It's yours. If it wanted me to put my hand into it, then the water would feel warm to me too.'

Merle realised that Junipa was right. Whether the hand that touched hers in the mirror belonged to one of her parents, or whether its fingers were those of someone else entirely – the fact was that it accepted only Merle. It might even be dangerous for someone else to reach so far into the space beyond the mirror.

The girls were still sitting side by side on the bed when the door opened and Eft came back. She had their supper on a wooden tray: good nourishing soup with vegetables and basil, white bread, and a jug of water from the cistern in the courtyard.

'Go to sleep when you've unpacked,' lisped the masked

woman as she left the room. 'You'll have all the time in the world to talk.'

Had Eft been eavesdropping on them? Did she know about the mirror under Merle's pillow? But Merle told herself she had no reason to suspect the housekeeper of anything; indeed, Eft had been very kind and friendly so far. The fact that she hid half her face behind a mask didn't make her a bad person.

She was still thinking of Eft's mask as she dropped off to sleep, and drowsily she wondered whether we don't all wear a mask at times.

A mask of happiness, a mask of grief, a mask of indifference.

A mask saying: now you don't see me.

MIRROR-GLASS EYES

In her dreams, Merle met the Flowing Queen.

She felt as if she were riding a creature made of soft glass through the waters of the lagoon. Phantom shapes, green and blue, surged around them, millions of drops as warm as the water inside her mirror. They caressed her cheeks, her throat, the palms of her hands as she held them out to the current. She felt she was at one with the Flowing Queen, a being as mysterious as sunrise, as the forces of thunder and the stormy wind, as hard to understand as life and death. They dived down below the surface of the water, but Merle had no difficulty in breathing, for the Queen was in her and kept her alive, as if they were both parts of a single body.

Shoals of glittering fish swam beside them, companions on their way. Merle felt that their destination was less and less important. It was the journey alone that mattered, her union with the Flowing Queen, the sense that she understood the lagoon and shared its beauty.

And although nothing else happened – she just went gliding along beside the Queen – Merle's dream was the loveliest she had dreamed for months, for years. Her nights in the orphanage had been nights of cold, of flea bites, and the fear of theft. But here, in Arcimboldo's house, she was safe at last.

Merle woke up. At first she thought some sound had roused her from sleep, but there was nothing. All was still.

The Flowing Queen. Everyone had heard of her, yet no one knew what she really was. When the Egyptian galleys, after waging wars of annihilation all over the world, tried to enter the Venetian lagoon, something strange had happened. Strange and wonderful: the Flowing Queen had put them to flight. The Egyptian Empire, the greatest, most cruel power in the history of the world, had been forced to turn tail and retreat.

Ever since then, legends had grown up around the Flowing Queen.

It was certain that she was not a creature of flesh and blood. She filled and pervaded the lagoon, the narrow canals of the city, the wide expanses of water between the islands. The Councillors claimed to hold regular conversations with her and carry out her wishes. But if she had ever really spoken, it was never in the presence of the common people.

Many said she was no bigger than a water drop, moving now here, now there; others swore she was the water itself, every little sip of it, however tiny. She was more a natural force than a living being, and some even saw her as a deity filling every created thing.

The tyrant's campaign might have left suffering, death and devastation in its wake, Amenophis and his empire might have subjugated the world – but the aura of the Flowing Queen had now protected the lagoon for over thirty years, and there wasn't a soul in the city who did not feel indebted to her. Mass was said in her honour in the churches, the fishermen offered her part of every catch, and even the secret Guild of Thieves showed its gratitude by keeping its quick fingers to itself on certain days in the year.

There – a sound again! This time there was no doubt about it.

Merle sat up in bed. The lingering remnants of the dream were still washing around in her mind, like sea spray breaking over your feet as you walk along a beach.

The sound was repeated. A metallic, grating noise, coming up from the courtyard. Merle knew that sound – it was the cistern lid. You heard it all over Venice when the heavy metal covers over the wells were opened. There were cisterns all over the city, in every public square and in most of the courtyards. Their round walls were ornamented with patterns and fabulous creatures carved in stone. The huge, semicircular covers protected the precious drinking water from dirt and rats.

But who could be taking the lid off a cistern at this time of night? Merle got up and rubbed the sleep from her eyes. Slightly unsteady on her legs, she went over to the window.

In the moonlight, she was just in time to see a figure climbing over the edge of the cistern and slipping into the dark shaft of the well. A moment later, hands rose from the darkness, grasped the edge of the lid, and pulled it back down over the opening. It closed with another grating sound.

Merle let out a sharp breath. She instinctively ducked, although the figure had disappeared down the well by now.

Eft! There was no doubt about it; she had been the shadowy figure down in the courtyard. But what made the housekeeper climb down a well in the middle of the night?

Merle swung round to wake Junipa.

Her bed was empty.

'Junipa?' she whispered tensely. But there was no corner of the little room that she couldn't see from here. No hiding place.

Unless . . .

Merle bent down and looked under the two beds. But she found no trace of the girl there either.

She went to the door. It had no bolt that they could put across it in the evening, no lock. Out in the corridor, silence reigned.

Merle took a deep breath. The floor beneath her bare feet was very cold. She quickly put on her dress and thrust her feet into her well-worn leather shoes. They came up over her ankles and had to be laced, which was going to take far too much time just now. But she couldn't go looking for Junipa and risk falling over her own shoelaces. She quickly set to work, but her fingers shook, and it took her twice as long as usual to do up her shoes.

At last she slipped out into the corridor and closed the door. Somewhere in the distance she heard a threatening hiss – not an animal sound, more like some steam-driven machine – but she wasn't sure whether whatever had made it was in this house. Soon she heard the hissing again, followed by a rhythmical pounding. Then there was silence again. Only when Merle was already on her way downstairs did she remember that there were only two inhabited houses on the Outcasts' Canal: Arcimboldo's mirror workshop, and the weaver's workshop on the opposite bank.

There was a strange smell all over the house, rather like a mixture of lubricating oil, polished steel, and the acrid odour she remembered from the glass-making workshops of the lagoon island of Murano; she had been there just once, when an old glass-blower had thought of taking her on as an apprentice. As soon as she arrived, he had told her to scrub his back in the bath. Merle waited until he was sitting in the water and then ran back to the quayside as fast as she could go. She had managed to get back to the city, hidden in one of the boats. Such cases were not unknown in the orphanage, and although the staff were by no means pleased to see her back they had the decency not to send her to Murano again.

Merle reached the landing on the second floor. So far she had met no one and seen no sign of life. Where did the other apprentices sleep? Presumably on the third floor, like Junipa and Merle herself. At least she knew that Eft wasn't in the house – and she avoided thinking too hard about what that strange woman might be doing down in the cistern.

That left Arcimboldo himself. And Junipa, of course.

Suppose she'd simply had to spend a penny? The narrow oriel window of the little room where a round hole in the floor sent its contents straight down into the canal was on the third floor too. Merle hadn't looked in there, and now she was kicking herself. She had forgotten the most obvious thing – perhaps because, at the orphanage, it was always a bad sign when children disappeared from their beds at night. Few of them were ever seen again.

She was just about to turn, go back, and look when the hissing came again. It still made an artificial, mechanical noise, and the sound made her shudder.

Briefly, only very briefly, she thought she could hear something else too, a very soft sound against the background of the hissing.

A sob.

Junipa!

Merle tried to make out her surroundings in the dark stairway. It was pitch black; only a faint moonbeam fell in through a tall window nearby, a vague suggestion of light, hardly enough to show her the steps beneath her feet. In the corridor to her left, a grandfather clock ticked all by itself in the shadows, a monstrous shape like a coffin propped against the wall.

By now she was sure that the hissing and sobbing came from inside the house. From further down. From the workshop on the first floor.

Merle hurried downstairs. The corridor leading away from the stairwell had a high, vaulted ceiling. She went along it as quickly and quietly as she could. Her throat felt tight. Her breath sounded as loud in her own ears as the clanking of the steamers on the Canal Grande. Suppose she and Junipa had simply jumped out of the frying pan into the fire? Suppose Arcimboldo turned out to be a monster like that old glass-blower on Murano?

She jumped when she saw something moving close to her. But it was only her own reflection flitting past one of the many mirrors on the walls.

The hissing noise came more frequently now, and it sounded closer. Eft hadn't shown them exactly where the entrance to the workshop was, saying only that it was on the first floor. But there were several doors here, all of them tall and dark, and all of them closed. Merle had no choice but to follow the sounds. She hadn't heard that soft sobbing again. The idea of Junipa helpless and delivered up to some unknown danger brought tears to Merle's eyes.

One thing was certain, anyway: she wasn't going to let

any harm come to her new friend, even if it meant that they were both sent back to a Home. She didn't want to think of a yet worse fate, but all the same, unpleasant ideas crept into her mind like little gnats, buzzing and stinging: *It's night. And it's dark. And any number of people have already disappeared in the canals. No one would bother about a pair of orphan girls. Just two mouths less to feed.*

The corridor made a right turn, and at the far end Merle saw the glowing outline of a double door rising to a pointed arch. The narrow gaps around the two sides of the door shone like gold wire held in a candle flame. A fierce fire must be burning inside the workshop – it would be the coal-burning furnace of the engine that made those primeval hissing, puffing sounds.

As Merle approached the door on tiptoe, she saw smoke covering the stone flags of the corridor like fog rising from the ground. The smoke was seeping out under the door, brightly lit by the flames inside the room.

Suppose the workshop was on fire? Keep calm, Merle kept telling herself. Keep perfectly, perfectly calm.

Her feet disturbed the smoke on the floor, conjuring up the shapes of misty ghosts in the darkness and casting distorted shadows on the walls, greatly enlarged shadows.

The only light was the glowing outline of the door.

Darkness, fog, the glowing door straight ahead of her. To Merle, it felt like being at the mouth of Hell, it was so unreal and oppressive.

The acrid smell she had noticed higher up on the stairs was even stronger here. So was the stink of oil. There were rumours that over the past few months envoys from Hell had visited the City Council, offering their master's aid in the struggle against the Empire. But the City Councillors had rejected the idea of any kind of pact with the Devil; they didn't need one while the Flowing Queen protected them all. Since 1833, when a National Geographic Society expedition led by the famous explorer, Professor Charles Burbridge, had discovered that Hell was a real place inside the earth, there had been several meetings between representatives of the human race and the envoys of Satan. But no one really knew very much about the subject, which was probably just as well.

All this passed through Merle's head as she took the last few steps up to the workshop door. Very, very cautiously she placed the palm of one hand against the wood. She expected it to feel hot, but she was proved wrong. The wood was cool, and in no way different from the other doors in the house.

The metal handle was cold too when Merle touched it.

She wondered whether she should just walk in. Well, it was all she could do. She was alone, and she doubted whether anyone in this house would come to her aid.

She had just made this decision when the handle on the other side of the door was pressed down. Merle spun round, ready to run, but then stepped back into the shelter of the left-hand side of the door while the right-hand side swung back into the room.

A broad beam of bright light flooded over the smoke on the floor. Where Merle had just been standing, its fumes were swept aside by the draught. Then a shadow fell over the beam of light. Someone was coming out into the corridor.

Merle pressed back as close as she could into the shelter of the left-hand side of the door. She was less than two metres away from the figure.

Shadows can make those who cast them look threatening even when, in reality, they are nothing of the kind. They make short people look tall and skinny people as broad as elephants. It was the same in this case.

The further the little old man moved away from the source of light, the more the mighty shadow shrank. He stood there without noticing Merle, a slightly ridiculous figure in trousers much too long for him, and a once white coat that was now nearly black with soot and smoke. His untidy grey hair stood out in all directions. His face was gleaming. A drop of sweat ran down his temple and into his bushy side-whiskers.

Instead of moving towards Merle, he turned back to the door and put his hand out towards the light. A second shadow joined his on the floor.

'Come, my child,' he said gently. 'Come out.'

Merle stood perfectly still. This was not the way she'd imagined her first meeting with Arcimboldo. Only the gentle calm in the old man's voice gave her a glimmer of hope.

But then the mirror-maker said, 'The pain will soon be gone.'

Pain?

'There's nothing to fear,' said Arcimboldo, still turned towards the open door. 'Believe me, you'll soon get used to it.'

Merle hardly dared to breathe.

Arcimboldo moved two or three paces down the corridor, walking backwards. As he did so he held out both hands, urging the person he had addressed to follow him.

'Come closer . . . yes, that's right. Very slowly.'

And Junipa came out. Taking small, uncertain steps, she walked through the door and out into the corridor. She was moving stiffly and with great caution.

But she can't see, thought Merle desperately. Why was Arcimboldo letting her wander around a place she didn't know, without help? Why didn't he wait until she could take his hand? Instead, he kept moving back, away from the door – and any moment now he would surely discover Merle, hidden in the shadows. As if spellbound, she stared at Junipa walking past her and down the corridor. Arcimboldo himself had eyes only for the girl.

'You're doing well,' he said encouragingly. 'Very, very well.'

The smoke low on the floor was gradually drifting away. No more came from the workshop. The glowing light of the flames bathed the corridor in wavering, dim, orange light.

'It's all so . . . blurred,' whispered Junipa pitifully.

Blurred? thought Merle in surprise.

'That will soon pass off,' said the mirror-maker. 'Just wait a little – in daylight tomorrow morning, everything will look different. You only have to trust me. Come a little closer.'

Junipa's footsteps were steadier now. Her careful gait was not because she couldn't see. Quite the opposite.

'What can you recognise?' asked Arcimboldo. 'What exactly?'

'I don't know. There's something moving.'

'Only shadows. Don't be afraid.'

Merle couldn't believe her ears. Was it possible, was it actually possible that Arcimboldo had restored Junipa's eyesight?

'I could never see at all before,' said Junipa, confused. 'I've been blind from birth.'

'Is the light you see red?' asked the mirror-maker.

'I don't know what light looks like,' she said uncertainly. 'And I don't know colours.'

Arcimboldo grimaced, as if annoyed with himself. 'Stupid of me. I should have thought of that.' He stopped and waited until he could take hold of Junipa's outstretched hands. 'You'll have much to learn in the next few weeks and months.'

'That's what I came here for.'

'Your life will change, now that you can see.'

Merle couldn't stay in hiding any longer. Ignoring any consequences, she came out of the shadows and into the light. 'What have you been doing to her?'

Arcimboldo glanced her way in surprise. Junipa blinked too. She was trying hard to make something out. 'Merle?' she asked.

'I'm here.' Merle moved to Junipa's side and gently touched her arm.

'Ah, our other new pupil.' Arcimboldo was quick to overcome his surprise. 'And rather an inquisitive one, it appears. But never mind. You'd have found out tomorrow morning anyway. So you're Merle.'

She nodded. 'And you're Arcimboldo.'

'Indeed I am.'

Merle looked away from the old mirror-maker and back at Junipa. She was not prepared for the full realisation of what he had done. At first glance and in the dim light she hadn't noticed the change, but now she wondered how she could have overlooked *that*. An icy hand seemed to be travelling down her back.

'But . . . but how . . .?'

Arcimboldo smiled proudly. 'Remarkable, isn't it?'

Merle could not utter a word. She stared silently at Junipa.

At her face.

At her eyes.

Junipa's blank eyeballs were gone. Instead, silver mirrors fitted into her eye sockets sparkled under her lids. They were not curved like an ordinary eyeball, but flat. Arcimboldo had replaced Junipa's eyes with splinters of a crystal mirror.

'What have you –'

Arcimboldo gently interrupted her. 'Done to her? Nothing, child. She can see again, a little anyway, but it will get better every day.'

'She has mirrors in her eyes!'

'That's right.'

'But . . . but that's . . .'

'Magic?' Arcimboldo shrugged his shoulders. 'Some might say so. Myself, I call it science. Apart from humans and animals, there's only one thing in the world that can see. Look in a mirror and it will look back at you. That's the first lesson to be learned in my workshop, Merle. Remember it well. Mirrors can see.'

'He's right, Merle,' Junipa agreed. 'I really can see something. And I feel as if I'm seeing a little more every minute.'

Arcimboldo nodded, pleased. 'Excellent!' He took Junipa's hand and did a little dance of glee with her, just carefully enough not to sweep her off her feet. The last wisps of the cloud of smoke swirled around them. 'Well, isn't it amazing?'

Merle stared at the two of them, still almost unable to believe her own eyes. Junipa, who had been blind from birth, could see. Thirteen years of darkness were over. And she owed it all to Arcimboldo, this thin little man with the untidy hair.

'Now, help your friend back to your room,' said the mirror-maker, when he had let go of Junipa. 'You both have a strenuous day ahead of you tomorrow. Well, every day in my workshop is strenuous. But I think you'll like it here. Oh yes, I really do.' He gave Merle his hand and added, 'Welcome to the house of Arcimboldo.'

Slightly dazed, she remembered what they had impressed upon her in the orphanage. 'Thank you very much for letting us come here,' she said politely. But she scarcely heard her own words. Bewildered, she watched the old man as he hurried back into his workshop with a satisfied look, tripping lightly along, and closed the double door behind him.

Hesitantly, Merle took Junipa's hand and helped her up the stairs to the third floor. Every few steps she asked, anxiously, if Junipa was sure it really didn't hurt too much. And whenever Junipa turned to her, Merle shivered slightly. For in those mirror-glass eyes she saw not her friend but only herself, reflected twice over and slightly distorted. She comforted herself by thinking that she only had to get used to it. The sight of Junipa would soon seem quite normal to her.

Yet one faint doubt remained. Before the change, Junipa's eyes had been blind and milky; now they were as cold as polished steel.

'I can see, Merle. I can really see.'

Junipa was still murmuring those words to herself long after they were back in bed again.

Only once, hours later, did Merle wake from confused dreams, when she heard the grating of the cistern cover again, down in the courtyard and very, very far away.

Their first few days in Arcimboldo's mirror-making workshop were tiring, for Merle and Junipa were given all the work the three older boy apprentices didn't want to do. Several times a day, Merle had to sweep up the fine ground glass that settled on the workshop floor like the desert sand which, in many a summer, drifted over the sea to Venice.

As Arcimboldo had promised, Junipa's eyesight improved daily. She could still see little more than vague outlines, but she was already able to tell things apart, and she was keen to find her way around the strange workshop without help. However, she was given work that was easier than Merle's, although not much more pleasant. She wasn't allowed any real chance to recover from the stress of that first night, and she had to weigh out endless quantities of quartz sand from sacks and pour it into measuring jugs. What exactly Arcimboldo did with it was still a mystery to the girls.

In fact Arcimboldo's mirror-making seemed to have little to do with the ancient traditions which had been the pride of Venice from time immemorial. Once, in the sixteenth century, only the chosen few had been taught the art of mirror-making. They were all under strict guard on the glass-blowers' island of Murano, where they lived in luxury and wanted for nothing – except their freedom. Once they began training they could never leave the island again, and anyone who tried must die. La Serenissima's agents hunted renegade mirror-makers right across Europe, striking the offenders down before they could pass on the secret of making mirrors to anyone else. Only the mirrors of Murano adorned the great noblemen's houses of Europe, for Venice alone knew the art of creating them. The secret was not to be bought from the city at any price – but it could be bought from individuals, and at last some mirror-makers did succeed in escaping from Murano and selling their secret art to the French. By way of thanks the French killed them, and soon opened workshops of their own, depriving Venice of its monopoly. Soon mirrors were being made in many countries, and the prohibitions and penalties imposed on the mirror-makers of Murano lapsed into oblivion.

But Arcimboldo's mirrors had as much to do with alchemy as with the art of glass-making, and after her first few days Merle began to realise that it might be years before he initiated her into their secrets. Even the three boys – the eldest, Dario, had already been in the house for more than two years – had not the faintest inkling of Arcimboldo's art. They had watched him, of course; they had eavesdropped and spied on him too, but they didn't know the real secret.

Lean, black-haired Dario was the leader of Arcimboldo's apprentices. He always behaved well in front of his master, but at heart he was still the same lout he had been when he arrived from the orphanage two years ago. During the apprentices' scanty leisure time he was boastful and sometimes tyrannical, but the other two boys suffered more from him than Merle and Junipa. Indeed, he preferred to ignore the girls most of the time. He didn't like the fact that Arcimboldo had taken on girl apprentices, probably because he wasn't on the best of terms with Eft. He seemed to fear that Merle and Junipa would take the housekeeper's side in any quarrel, or they might give away some of his little secrets to her – such as the way he regularly drank Arcimboldo's good red wine, even though Eft kept it under lock and key. She didn't suspect that Dario had worked hard to make another key to the kitchen dresser. Merle had discovered Dario's thieving ways by chance on her third night, when she met him in the dark of the corridor with a jug full of wine. It would never have crossed her mind to use what she had seen to her own advantage, but that was obviously what Dario feared. From then on he had been even cooler towards her, indeed hostile, although he dared not pick an open quarrel. Most of the time he ignored her – which, strictly speaking, was more attention than he paid to Junipa, who might not have existed at all as far as he was concerned.

Secretly Merle wondered why Arcimboldo had ever taken on the rebellious Dario as an apprentice. But that brought up the uncomfortable question of what he saw in *her*, and so far no answer had occurred to her. Junipa might be an ideal guinea pig for his experiment with those shards of mirror-glass – by now the girls had discovered that he had never tried anything like that before – but what had prompted him to free Merle from the orphanage? He had never met her, he must have relied entirely on what the staff there said about her – and Merle doubted that much of what Arcimboldo heard was good. She had been considered rebellious in the Home, a cheeky brat – terms used by the staff for anyone who was eager to learn and self-confident.

The other two boy apprentices were only a year older than Merle. One, a pale-faced, red-headed boy, was called Tiziano; the other – skinnier and with a slight harelip – was Boro. They both seemed pleased not to be the youngest any more and to have Merle to order about, although their bossiness never turned to unkindness. If they saw that her work was too much for her, they willingly lent a hand, unasked. But they seemed to think Junipa uncanny, and even Boro preferred to steer clear of her. The boys accepted

Dario as their leader; they didn't fawn on him the way Merle had seen in some gangs in the orphanage, but they obviously looked up to him. He had been Arcimboldo's apprentice a year longer than either of them, after all.

When she had been there about a week and a half, Merle saw Eft climbing down the well again just before twelve one night. She wondered briefly whether to wake Junipa, but then decided not to. She stood motionless at the window for a while, staring at the cover of the cistern, and then lay down in bed again, feeling uneasy.

She had already told Junipa about her discovery on one of their first evenings in Arcimboldo's house.

'She really climbed into the cistern?' Junipa had asked.

'I told you she did!'

'Perhaps the rope of the bucket had broken?'

'Would you go climbing down a dark well in the middle of the night just for a broken rope? If that was all, she could have done it in daylight. Anyway, one of us would have been sent to do the job.' Merle shook her head firmly. 'She didn't even have a lantern with her.'

Junipa's mirror-glass eyes reflected the moonlight falling in through the window that evening. They looked as if they were radiating white, icy light. As so often, Merle had to suppress a shudder. At such moments she sometimes felt that Junipa saw more with her new eyes than just the surface of people and things – it was almost as if she could look straight into Merle's mind.

'Are you afraid of Eft?' asked Junipa.

Merle thought for a moment. 'No. But you have to admit that she's strange.'

'Perhaps we'd all be strange if we had to wear a mask.'

'Why does she wear it, anyway? No one but Arcimboldo seems to know. I even asked Dario.'

'Perhaps you'd just better ask Eft herself.'

'That would be rude if she really does have some skin disease.'

'What else could it be?'

Merle didn't reply. She had often asked herself the same question. She did have a suspicion, only a vague one, but, once it had occurred to her, she couldn't get it out of her head. All the same, she thought it would be better not to confide it to Junipa.

Merle and Junipa hadn't discussed Eft again since that evening. There was so much else to talk about, so many new impressions, discoveries, challenges. For Junipa in particular, with her rapidly improving eyesight, every day was a new adventure. Merle envied her slightly for the easy enthusiasm she could summon up for the smallest things, but she rejoiced with her friend over the unexpected cure for her blindness.

On the morning after the night when Merle had seen Eft climb down into the well for the second time, something happened to take her mind off the housekeeper's secret expeditions. The girls had their first encounter with the apprentices from the other bank of the canal, the pupils of Umberto the master weaver.

During the eleven days Merle had now spent in the mirror-maker's house she had almost forgotten the weaver's workshop across the canal. There had been no sign of the notorious dispute between the two masters that was once the talk of all Venice. And Merle hadn't left the house at all in those eleven days. She spent most of her time in the workshop, the storerooms next to it, the dining room or the girls' bedroom. Now and then one of the apprentices had to go to the vegetable market on the Rio San Barnabo with Eft, but so far the housekeeper had always chosen one of the boys. They were bigger and could carry the heavy crates easily.

So Merle was taken entirely by surprise when the

apprentices on the other side of the canal made their presence emphatically felt. As she discovered later, it had been traditional for many years for the pupils of both houses to play tricks on each other, and these brawls often ended with broken windowpanes, angry masters, bruises and grazes. The last such attack had been three weeks ago, and it was the doing of Dario, Boro and Tiziano. High time, then, for the weaver's boys to strike back.

Merle didn't know why they had chosen this particular morning, nor was she sure how the weaver's apprentices got into the house – although later she suspected that they had put a plank over the canal from one balcony to the other and simply walked over it to the mirror-maker's side. All this took place in the morning, in broad daylight and thus during working hours, which showed that it was done with Umberto's blessing, just as earlier attacks by Dario and the others had been carried out by agreement with Arcimboldo.

Merle was just gluing the wooden frame on to a mirror when she heard a loud crash near the workshop door. She looked up in alarm, fearing that Junipa had stumbled over a tool.

But it wasn't Junipa. A small figure had slipped on a

screwdriver and was struggling to keep its balance, staggering about. Its face was hidden behind a bear mask made of glazed paper. One hand was flailing in the air, while the paint bomb it had been holding in the other splashed on the flagstones like a blue star.

'*Weavers!*' shouted Tiziano, leaving his work and jumping up.

'Weavers! Weavers!' In another corner of the room, Boro took up his friend's cry, and soon Dario came running up too.

Merle rose from her seat, confused. Her glance wandered aimlessly round the room. She didn't understand what was going on; no one had told her about the feud between the apprentices.

The masked figure at the entrance slipped on the paint he had spilled and landed on the seat of his trousers. Before Dario and the others could mock him or maybe attack him, three more boys appeared in the corridor, all wearing brightly coloured painted masks. One in particular caught Merle's attention: it was the face of a magnificent fabulous animal, half man, half bird. The long hooked beak was lacquered gold, and tiny glass stones glittered in the painted eyebrows.

Merle never got round to looking at the other masks, because a whole cluster of paint bombs was flying her way. One burst at her feet, splashing them with sticky red, another hit her shoulder and bounced off without breaking. It rolled away towards Junipa, who was standing with a broom of birch twigs in her hand, bewildered by what was going on. Now, however, she quickly took in the situation, bent down, picked up the paint bomb and flung it back at the intruders. The boy with the bear mask jumped aside, and her throw hit the bird-faced lad behind him. The paint bomb broke on the tip of the bird's beak, showering the wearer of the mask with green paint.

Dario crowed with delight, and Tiziano clapped Junipa encouragingly on the shoulder. Then came the second wave of the attack. This time they didn't get off so lightly. Boro, Tiziano and Merle herself were hit and splashed all over with paint. Out of the corner of her eye Merle saw Arcimboldo cursing as he closed the door of the mirror storeroom and bolted it from the inside. Never mind if his pupils came to blows – the completed magic mirrors must not be harmed.

The apprentices were left to their own devices. Four against four. Or five against four, if you counted Junipa –

after all, in spite of her weak eyes she had scored the first direct hit for the mirror-makers.

'It's the weaver's pupils from the opposite bank,' Boro shouted to Merle as he snatched up a broom, grasping it in both hands like a sword. 'We must defend the workshop at all costs!'

Typical boys, thought Merle, brushing rather helplessly at the paint on her dress. Why did they always have to do such silly things to prove themselves?

She looked up – and was hit on the forehead by another paint bomb. Sticky yellow poured over her face and shoulders.

That did it! With a cry of fury she snatched up the bottle of glue she had been using to stick the mirror frame in place, and made for the nearest weaver's apprentice. It was the boy with the bear mask. He saw her coming and tried to take another paint bomb out of the bag slung over his shoulder. Too late! Merle had reached him, hit him and flung him backwards; she dropped to her knees on his chest and pushed the narrow end of the glue bottle into the left-hand eye slit in the mask.

'Close your eyes!' she warned, squeezing a hefty jet of glue under the mask. The boy swore, but then his words were lost in gurgling, followed by a long drawn-out 'Yuuuukkk!'

Seeing that her adversary was out of action for the time being, she pushed herself away from him and jumped backwards, rising to her feet. She was now holding the glue bottle like a pistol – not that that made much sense, because there wasn't much glue left in it. Out of the corner of her eye she saw Boro and Tiziano wrestling with two weaver's boys in a fierce combat; the mask worn by one of the weaver's apprentices had already broken apart. But instead of intervening, Merle ran over to Junipa, seized her by the arm and pulled her down into shelter behind one of the workbenches.

'Stay here and don't move!' she told her.

Junipa protested. 'I'm not as helpless as you think.'

'No, I know.' Merle cast a smiling glance at the boy with the bird mask. His chest was green from Junipa's paint bomb. 'All the same – better stay under cover. This can't go on much longer.'

But when she got to her feet she saw that she had spoken too soon. Tiziano's opponents had the upper hand again. And there was no sign of Dario. Merle didn't see him until he suddenly appeared in the doorway with a knife glinting in his hand, one of the knives Arcimboldo generally used to cut the thin silver plating for the backs of the mirrors. Its blade was not long, but it was razor-sharp.

'Serafin!' Dario called to the boy with the bird mask. 'Come here if you dare.'

The weaver's boy saw the knife in Dario's hand and braced himself for the challenge. His three companions retreated to the door, while Boro first helped Tiziano to his feet and then pushed Merle over to the wall of the workshop.

'Are they crazy?' she said breathlessly. 'They'll kill each other.'

Boro's frown showed that he shared her anxiety. 'Dario and Serafin have hated each other ever since they first met. Serafin's the leader of the weavers. He thought all this up.'

'That's no reason to go at him with a knife.'

While they were talking, Dario and Serafin had met in the middle of the room. It struck Merle that Serafin moved as nimbly as a dancer. He skilfully avoided Dario's crude blows, while the knife cut silvery trails in the air. Before Dario knew it, the weaver's apprentice had forced the knife from his hand. Dario fell on his adversary with a cry of fury and struck him a nasty blow on the throat. The yellow bird mask flew off and showed Serafin's face. His cheekbones were thin and high, his nose sprinkled with a few freckles. He had fair hair, though not as pale as Junipa's, and it was full of sticky green paint.

The light-blue eyes of the weaver's apprentice were narrowed in anger and, before Dario could duck, Serafin had struck a blow that sent the mirror-maker's pupil reeling back against the workbench where Junipa was sheltering. Dario leaped over the bench to get it between him and his opponent. Scared, Junipa took a step back. But Serafin was following Dario and was about to seize him again. Dario's nose was bleeding. That last thrust had weakened him. Instead of facing his adversary, he swung round, seized the surprised Junipa by her shoulders with both hands, hauled her roughly out in front of him and gave her a powerful shove that sent her stumbling in Serafin's direction.

Merle uttered a cry of fury. 'The coward!'

The weaver's apprentice saw Junipa coming, with Dario following her to make the best use of this chance. Serafin had a choice: he could catch Junipa to prevent her from colliding with a shelf full of glass bottles – or he could dodge her and defend himself against his arch-enemy.

Serafin reached for Junipa and managed to get hold of her, and for a split second he held her in an embrace meant to protect and soothe her. 'It's all right,' he whispered. 'Nothing's going to happen to you.'

No sooner had he said these words than Dario rammed his fist over Junipa's shoulder straight into Serafin's face.

'No!' cried Merle indignantly. She raced past Boro and Tiziano, ran round the workbench and hauled Dario away from Serafin and Junipa.

'What are you doing?' snapped the older boy, but she had already flung him backwards to the floor.

Her glance briefly met Serafin's as he carefully put Junipa aside. His face was smeared with green paint and blood, but he was smiling. Then he made haste to rejoin his friends at the entrance.

'Well, we'll be off,' he said, and a moment later the weaver's apprentices had gone.

Merle took no notice of Dario, but turned to Junipa, who was standing in front of the shelf of bottles. 'Everything all right?'

Junipa nodded. 'Yes . . . yes, thanks. I'm fine.'

Behind Merle's back, Dario began cursing and swearing. She felt him coming dangerously close to her. Abruptly, she spun round, looked deep into his narrow eyes, and slapped his face as hard as she could.

In a flash, before Dario could attack her, Eft was between them. Merle felt her powerful grasp as the housekeeper grabbed her by the shoulder and pulled her away from Dario. But she didn't hear what Eft was saying, or Dario's angry insults. He didn't seem able to calm down. Thoughtfully, she looked out at the corridor down which Serafin and his friends had disappeared.

EFT'S STORY

'So what, I wonder, am I to do with you young people?'

The Master's voice sounded more disappointed than angry. Arcimboldo was sitting at his desk in the library. The walls of the room were lined with leather-bound books. Merle wondered whether he had really read them all.

'The harm done by the weaver's apprentices throwing paint about is nothing to the damage you two did,' Arcimboldo went on, allowing his gaze to move from Dario to Merle and back again. They stood in front of the table, looking at the floor and feeling embarrassed. Their anger with each other had by no means died down, but even Dario seemed to realise that it would be better to keep quiet. 'You encouraged a fight among the apprentices. And you made the others take sides. If Eft hadn't intervened, Junipa, Boro and Tiziano would have had to decide to back one or other of you.' There was an angry glitter in the old man's eyes. He looked stern and unapproachable now. 'I can't have my pupils on bad terms. I want them working well together and avoiding any unnecessary conflicts. Magic mirrors need to mature in a special kind of harmonious atmosphere. If there's hostility in the air, a shadow falls on the glass, dims it and makes it blank.'

Merle felt that he wasn't telling the truth. He wanted to make them feel guilty. It would have suited him better not to sound so angry about 'unnecessary conflicts'. After all, it was his own childish argument with Umberto that had caused all the trouble in the first place.

Sooner or later she and Dario would have been at odds in any case, she'd sensed that on the very first day. She guessed that Arcimboldo had foreseen it too. Was he regretting taking her out of the orphanage? Would she have to go back to dirt and poverty now?

In spite of her fears, she did not feel guilty. Dario was a miserable coward, and he'd shown that twice already: first when he went for Serafin with that knife, and second when he took refuge behind the defenceless Junipa. He thoroughly deserved to have his face slapped, and if it had been up to her, that would have been followed by a good thrashing.

Arcimboldo clearly felt much the same. 'Dario,' he said, 'you'll clean the workshop by yourself as punishment for your unworthy and improper conduct, and I don't want to see a single speck of paint left tomorrow morning, understand?'

'So what about her?' grumbled Dario, looking furiously at Merle.

'I asked if you understood me,' Arcimboldo said again, his bushy eyebrows coming together like two thunder-clouds.

Dario bowed his head, although it did not escape Merle that he was surreptitiously giving her an angry glare. 'Yes, Master.'

'Dario will need a great deal of water, so you, Merle, will draw ten buckets of water from the cistern, and then carry them upstairs and into the workshop. That will be *your* punishment.'

'But Master –' protested Dario.

Arcimboldo interrupted him. 'Your conduct has put us all to shame, Dario. I know you're hot-headed and quick-tempered, but you are also my best pupil, so I'll leave it at that. As for Merle, she's only been with us for two weeks and has yet to learn that arguments here, in contrast to the orphanage, are not conducted by physical violence. Have I made myself sufficiently clear?'

Both young people bowed and said, in unison, 'Yes, Master.'

'Any objections?'

'No, Master.'

'Very well.' He waved a hand, indicating that they might leave.

Outside the library door, Merle and Dario exchanged dark looks, and then they both turned to their appointed tasks. As Dario set about clearing away the aftermath of the paint-bomb attack in the workshop, Merle went down to the courtyard. A dozen wooden buckets stood by the back door. She picked up the first and went to the cistern.

Strange creatures carved from stone were set into the wall around the well, fantastic beings with cats' eyes, the heads of Gorgons and reptilian tails. They formed a procession, frozen motionless in their progress round the cistern, led by a creature, half-human, half-shark, with arms that had elbows pointing the wrong way. It carried a human head in its hands.

The metal cover of the well was heavy. Merle managed to open it only with much grunting and groaning. All seemed black underneath the lid. Only deep, deep below did she see a faint shimmer of light, reflecting the sky above the courtyard.

She turned and looked up. The view above was not very

different from the inside of the cistern: the walls of the old buildings rose like ramparts around the courtyard. Perhaps the water down below wasn't quite as deep as she had thought, but the shaft of the well seemed more than twice its real depth because it reflected the height of the yard. It would be less difficult to climb down to the surface than Merle had thought – particularly as she could now see metal handholds and footholds inside the well leading to the depths below. What sent Eft down there again and again?

Merle tied the bucket to a long rope lying ready beside the cistern and let it down. The wood scraped against the stone side of the well. The sound echoed in the depths and came up to daylight again distorted, sounding almost like a whisper from the mouths that were the building's windows. The voices of all who had lived here long ago. The whispering of ghosts.

Merle couldn't see when the bucket reached the surface of the water. It was too dark down there. But she did see the reflection of the sky in the well suddenly begin to move; the bucket had probably dipped into the water. The only strange thing was that she felt the pull of the rope still going down, and the scraping against the stone wall sounded the same too. If it wasn't the bucket churning up the surface of the water, then what was it?

She had scarcely asked herself that question before something emerged at the bottom of the shaft. A head. It was too far away for her to make out any details, yet she was sure that dark eyes were looking up at her.

In alarm, Merle let go of the rope and stepped back. The rope shot over the edge of the well and down to the depths. Both it and the bucket would have been lost if a hand had not unexpectedly reached out and grabbed it.

Eft's hand.

Merle had not noticed the housekeeper joining her in the yard. Eft had caught the end of the rope just in time, and now she hauled the bucket back up into the light of day.

'Thank you – th-that was clumsy of me,' Merle stammered.

'What did you see?' asked Eft, behind her half-mask.

'Nothing.'

'Please don't lie to me.'

Merle hesitated. Eft was still pulling up the bucket. Merle instinctively entertained the idea of turning and running away. That was what she'd have done a few weeks ago in the orphanage. But here something in her rebelled against the idea of giving in. She'd done nothing wrong or forbidden.

'There was something down there.'

'Yes?'

'A face.'

The housekeeper pulled the full bucket up out of the well and put it down on the surrounding wall. Water slopped over the rim and ran down the faces of the strange creatures on the stone relief.

'A face. Are you quite sure?' And then, sighing, Eft answered the question herself. 'Of course you are.'

'I did see it.' Merle wasn't sure how to behave. She felt that the housekeeper was very strange, yet she wasn't really afraid of her. It was more a kind of uneasiness about the way she looked over the top of her mask and seemed able to guess Merle's thoughts from every movement she made, every hesitation, however small.

'You've seen something before, haven't you?' Eft leaned against the wall of the well. 'The other night, for instance.'

There was no point in denying it. 'I heard the sound of the cover coming off. And then I saw you climb into the cistern.'

'Did you tell anyone?'

'No,' she lied, to keep Junipa out of it.

Eft passed a hand over her hair and sighed deeply. 'Merle,

there are a few things I must explain to you.'

'If you want to.'

'You're not like the other apprentices,' said the housekeeper. Was there a smile in her eyes? 'Not like Dario. You can cope with the truth.'

Merle came closer to Eft, so close that she could have put out her arm and touched the white mask with the red lips. 'You want to tell me a secret?'

'If you're ready for it.'

'But you don't know me at all.'

'Perhaps I know you better than you think.'

Merle didn't understand what Eft meant by that. Her curiosity was aroused now, and she wondered whether that was perhaps just what Eft intended. The more interested Merle was, the deeper she would be drawn into whatever was going on, and the sooner Eft could trust her.

'Come with me,' said the housekeeper, and she walked away from the well towards the back door of an empty house. It was not locked, and when Eft had pushed it open they were in a narrow corridor. Obviously it had once been the servants' entrance of this palazzo.

They passed a deserted kitchen with empty larders, and finally reached a short flight of stairs leading down –

unusual in a city where the houses were built on piles and very seldom had cellars.

A little later, Merle realised that Eft had brought her to an underground landing stage for boats. A path ran beside a channel of water that disappeared into semicircular tunnels on both sides of the moorings. Cargoes had once been loaded on boats here. There was a brackish smell in the air, an odour of seaweed and mould.

'Why don't you go down to the water this way?' asked Merle.

'What do you mean?'

'You climb down into the well because you want to go somewhere. Of course there could be a secret passage off to one side of the well-shaft, but to be honest I doubt it. I think it's the water itself attracting you.' She paused for a moment, and then added, 'You're a mermaid, aren't you?'

If Eft was surprised, she didn't show it. Merle knew exactly what she was saying, and she knew how absurd it must sound. For Eft had legs, shapely, human legs, unlike any other mermaid ever known. A mermaid's hips ended in a broad fish-tail.

Eft put both hands behind her head and carefully

removed the mask that covered the lower half of her face both day and night.

'You're not afraid of me, are you?' she asked. The corners of her wide mouth ended just a finger's breadth in front of her ears. She had no lips, but when she spoke folds of skin drew back, revealing several rows of small, sharp teeth.

'No,' replied Merle, and it was the truth.

'Good.'

'Are you going to tell me about it?'

'What do you want to know?'

'Why you don't come this way when you meet the other mermaids by night. Why do you risk being seen climbing down into the well?'

Eft narrowed her eyes, but what would have been an unspoken threat in a human being was only an expression of distaste in her. 'Because the water's contaminated. It's the same in all the canals of the city. It is poisonous, it's fatal to us. That's why so few of us come to Venice of our own free will. The water of the canals kills us, slowly but with absolute certainty.'

'The mermaids who pull the boats –'

'Will die. Every one of us that you humans catch and imprison or misuse in your games will die. The poison in the water corrodes first the skin and then the mind. Not even the Flowing Queen can save us.'

Deeply shocked, Merle was struck dumb. All the people who kept mermaids as pets for fun were murderers. Many of them must know what captivity in the canals did to the merfolk.

Ashamed, she looked Eft squarely in the eye. She had difficulty uttering any sound at all. 'I've never caught a mermaid.'

Eft smiled, showing her needle-sharp teeth again. 'I know. I can feel it. You have been touched by the Flowing Queen.'

'Me?'

'Weren't you taken out of the water when you were a baby?'

'You were listening to me and Junipa on our first evening, up in our room.' With anyone else she would have been indignant, but in Eft's case she felt it didn't matter.

'Yes, I was listening,' the mermaid admitted. 'So, since I know your secret, I'll tell you mine. That's only fair. And just as I will not tell yours to anyone else, you will keep silent about my own story.'

Merle nodded. 'What did you mean just now – about the Flowing Queen touching me?'

'You were set adrift on the canals. That happens to many children. But very few survive, most of them drown. However, you were found. The current bore you up, which can only mean that the Flowing Queen was looking after you.'

To Merle, it sounded as if Eft had actually been there, such was the conviction in her words. She thought that perhaps the mermaids worshipped the Flowing Queen as a goddess. Following this train of thought, Merle shivered: suppose the Queen didn't protect the human beings of the lagoon? After all, mermaids were water creatures and, if you believed some theories, then the Queen *was* the water. The unfathomable force of the sea.

'What is the Flowing Queen?' She didn't really expect Eft to know the answer to this question.

'If that was ever known, it's been long forgotten,' replied the mermaid quietly. 'Just as you and I and the Queen herself will be forgotten some day.'

'But we all venerate the Flowing Queen. Everyone in Venice loves her. She saved us all. No one can ever forget that.'

Eft merely shrugged her shoulders slightly, in silence, but Merle could tell that she didn't agree. The mermaid pointed to a slender gondola lying on the black water, tied to the moorings. It looked as if it were floating in a void, so smooth and dark was the surface of the water around it.

'We're getting in that boat?' asked Merle.

Eft nodded.

'And then?'

'I want to show you something.'

'Will we be gone very long?'

'An hour at the most.'

'Arcimboldo will punish me. He told me to bring the buckets –'

'Oh, that's been dealt with.' Eft smiled. 'He told me what he planned for the two of you, and I left ten full buckets ready in the workshop.'

Merle wasn't convinced. 'What about Dario?'

'He'll keep quiet. Or Arcimboldo will learn who steals his wine at night.'

'You know about that?'

'I know everything that goes on in this house.'

Merle hesitated no longer, but followed Eft into the gondola. The mermaid untied the rope, placed herself in the prow of the boat and steered it with the long oar towards one of the two openings into the tunnel. It was very dark around them.

'Don't worry,' said Eft. 'There's a torch in front of you, and tinder and flint beside it.'

Before long Merle had the pitch-soaked torch burning. The yellow, flickering light of its flame wandered over a tiled and vaulted roof.

'Can I ask you something?'

'You want to know why I have legs instead of a *kalimar*.'

'Kali-what?'

'*Kalimar*. That's what we call our fish-tails in our own language.'

'Will you tell me?'

Eft let the gondola glide further along in the darkness of the tunnel. Musty, ragged moss had come loose from the roof above and was hanging down like frayed draperies. The place smelled of rotting seaweed and decay.

'It's a sad story,' said Eft at last, 'so I'll make it short.'

'I like sad stories.'

'You may yet be the heroine of one yourself.' The mermaid turned to Merle and looked at her.

'Why do you say that?' asked Merle.

'You have been touched by the Flowing Queen,' Eft repeated, as if that was explanation enough. She sat up very straight, looking ahead of the gondola again. Her expression was grave. 'Once upon a time a mermaid was washed up on the shore of an island by a storm. She was so weak that she lay helpless among the reeds. The clouds drifted apart, the sun burned down, the mermaid's body dried out and turned brittle, and she began to die. But then a young man appeared, the son of a merchant whose father had given him the thankless task of trading with the few fisherfolk who lived on that island. He had spent all day with those poverty-stricken families, and they had shared their water and fish with him but had bought nothing, for they had no money and nothing worth bartering for his wares. Soon the young merchant's son was on his way back to his boat, but he dared not face his father after failing to sell anything. He feared what the merchant would say, for this wasn't the first time he had come home to Venice without making a profit, and he feared even more for his inheritance. His father was a stern, hard-hearted man who did not feel for the poverty of the people living on the outlying islands – indeed, he felt for nothing in the world except making money.

'So the young man was strolling aimlessly along the shore to the harbour where his boat lay, merely to delay his homecoming. As he wandered among the reeds and tall grass, lost in thought, he came upon the stranded mermaid.

He knelt down beside her, looked into her eyes, and fell in love with her on the spot. He didn't see the fish-tail below her hips, he didn't see the teeth that would have terrified anyone else. He only looked into her eyes as they gazed helplessly up at him, and he instantly made his decision: this was the woman he loved and wanted to marry. He carried her back to the water, and as she gradually recovered her strength in the breakers by the shore he spoke to her of love. The longer she listened to him the more she liked him. Liking turned to affection, and affection turned to something more. They promised to see each other again, and the very next day they met on the shore of another island, and the day after that on another island again, and so it went on.

'After a few weeks the young man summoned up all his courage and asked if she would follow him to the city. But she knew what happened to mermaids in the city, so she said no. He promised to make her his wife so that she could live with him like a human being. "But look at me," she said. "I shall never be like a human being." Then they were both very sad, and the young man saw that his plan had been nothing but a beautiful dream.

'The next night, however, the mermaid remembered the

legend of a powerful sea-witch who was said to live in an underwater cave far out in the Adriatic. So she swam out, further out than she or any of her mermaid companions had ever swum before, and she found the sea-witch sitting on a rock far below the surface of the water, looking for drowned men. For sea-witches, you see, eat carrion, and they like it best when it is old and bloated. The mermaid had passed a sunken fishing-boat on her way, so she was able to bring the witch a particularly tasty morsel as a gift. That put the old witch in a good mood. She listened to the mermaid's story and, probably still exhilarated by the taste of death, she decided to help her. She cast a spell and told the mermaid to go back to the lagoon. Once there, she was to lie down on the shore near the city and sleep until day dawned. Then, the witch promised, she would have legs instead of a tail. "But as for your mouth," she added, "I can't change that without leaving you mute for ever."

'The mermaid did not think her mouth was important, for after all it was part of the face that the merchant's son had fallen in love with. So she did as the sea-witch told her.

'She was found next morning at a harbour by the sea and, sure enough, she had legs where her fish-tail had once been. But the men who found her crossed themselves, said this was the Devil's work and beat her, recognising her as what she really was by her mouth. They felt sure that mermaids had found a way to turn into human beings, and they were afraid they would soon attack the city, murder its inhabitants and steal their wealth.

'What folly! As if any mermaid had ever thought anything of human riches!

'As the men hit and kicked her, the mermaid kept whispering her lover's name, so they soon sent for him. He came in haste with his father, who suspected some plot against him and his family. The mermaid and the young man were faced with each other, and they looked long and deep into one another's eyes. The young man wept, and the mermaid too shed tears that mingled with the blood on her cheeks. But then her lover turned away, for he was weak and feared his father's anger. "I don't know her," he said, repudiating her. "I have nothing to do with this monster."

'The mermaid fell silent and said no more, even when they beat her harder, and she still said nothing when the merchant and his son kicked her in the face and in the ribs with their boots. Later, she was thrown back into the water like a dead fish, and that was what they all thought her: dead.'

Eft fell silent, and for a moment she held the oar motionless in her hands without dipping it into the water. The light of the torch shone on her cheeks, and a single tear ran down her face. She was not telling some other mermaid's story, but her own.

'A child found her, an apprentice boy in a mirror-making workshop, taken from an orphanage by his master. The boy looked after the mermaid, hid her, brought her food and drink and kept giving her new courage when she wanted to end her own life. That boy's name was Arcimboldo, and the grateful mermaid promised to follow him all her life. Mermaids live much longer than you human beings, so today the boy is an old man while the mermaid is still young. She will be young when he dies too, and then she will be all alone again, a solitary creature between two worlds, not a mermaid now and not a human being either.'

When Merle looked at her, the tear on Eft's cheek had dried. And now it seemed once again as if she had been telling someone else's story, a story far away and unimportant. Merle would have liked to rise from where she sat and take her in her arms, but she knew that Eft expected no such thing, and probably wouldn't have liked it.

'Only a story,' whispered the mermaid. 'As true and as

false as all the other stories we wish we had never heard.'

'I'm glad you told me.'

Eft nodded very slightly, and then looked up and pointed, showing Merle their way ahead. 'Look,' she said. 'We're nearly there.'

The torchlight around them was not so bright now, although the flames still burned. It took a moment for Merle to realise that they had left the walls of the tunnel behind. The gondola had glided soundlessly into an underground room or cavern.

A slope emerged from the darkness ahead of them. It rose from the water, a steep gradient covered with something that Merle couldn't identify from a distance. Plants, perhaps. Pale, intertwining branches. But what plants of that size could grow and flourish down here?

Once, as they were crossing the dark lake that was the floor of this great hall, she thought she saw movements in the water. She persuaded herself that the movements were made by fish. Very large fish.

'There's no mountain anywhere for miles,' she said, speaking her thoughts aloud. 'So how can there be a cave in the middle of Venice?' She knew enough about the way the water level worked to be sure that they couldn't be *under* the sea. Whatever kind of hall this was, it lay in the middle of the city, among magnificent palaces and elegant facades – and it was not natural but artificially made.

'Who built this place?' she asked.

'A friend of the mermaids.' Eft's tone showed that she did not want to talk about it.

A place like this in the middle of the city! If it really was above the ground, it must have a disguised exterior somewhere. Disguised as what? The derelict palazzo of a noble family, now long forgotten? A huge complex of storerooms? There was no window giving any clue to what lay outside, and neither the roof nor the side walls could be made out in the dark. Only that strange slope, coming closer and closer.

Now Merle saw that her original doubts had been right. No plants grew on the slope. The branching structures were something else.

She suddenly caught her breath as she realised the truth.

They were bones. The bones of hundreds of mermaids. They lay piled on one another, twining together, forged together by death, tilting all ways in confusion. With her heart racing, Merle saw that their upper bodies were like human skeletons, while the remnants of their tails resembled outsize fish bones. The sight was both absurd and shocking.

'Did they all come here to die?'

'Of their own free will, yes,' said Eft, steering the gondola to the left so that the starboard side was level with the mountain of bones.

The torchlight simulated movement where there was none among the branching bones. The thin shadows twitched and quivered, moved like spiders' legs that had separated from their bodies and were now scurrying around one another of their own accord.

'The mermaids' graveyard,' whispered Merle. Everyone knew the old legend, but until now it had been thought that the graveyard lay somewhere near the outskirts of the lagoon or out in the middle of the sea. Treasure-seekers and adventurers had tried to find it, for the bones of a mermaid were harder and worth more than ivory, and in the old days they had been used to make fearsome weapons for use in single combat. It was difficult to take in the fact that the graveyard lay here in the city, right in front of the eyes of all Venetians. And Eft said a human had helped to build it too. What made him do it? And who had he been?

'I wanted you to see this place.' Eft inclined her head

slightly, and only after a moment did Merle understand that the gesture was meant for her. 'A secret for a secret. Never to be told. Sealed by the oath of one who has been touched by the Flowing Queen.'

'I'm to swear an oath?'

Eft nodded.

Merle didn't know exactly what to do, but she raised one hand and said solemnly: 'I swear an oath on my life never to tell anyone about the mermaids' graveyard.'

'An oath as one touched by the Flowing Queen,' Eft prompted her.

'I, Merle, touched by the Flowing Queen, swear this oath.'

Satisfied, Eft nodded, and Merle breathed a sigh of relief.

The hull of the gondola was scraping over something lying below the surface. 'More bones,' explained Eft. 'Thousands of bones.' She turned the gondola and steered it back towards the exit from the tunnel.

'Eft.'

'Yes?'

'You really do think I'm someone special, don't you?'

The mermaid smiled in a mysterious way. 'You are indeed. Very special.'

Much later, in bed in the dark, Merle put her arm into the water of her mirror under the covers, enjoying the pleasant warmth and feeling for the hand on the other side. She had to wait for quite a while, but then something touched her fingers, something very gentle, very familiar. Merle sighed faintly and fell into a light, uneasy sleep.

Outside the window, the evening star rose. Its sparkling light was reflected in Junipa's open mirror eyes as their chilly, fixed gaze stared through the dark room.

TREACHERY

'Have you ever looked right into it?' Junipa asked in the morning, when Eft had woken them by striking the gong down in the hall.

Merle rubbed the drowsiness from her eyes with the knuckles of her forefingers. 'Looked into what?'

'Your water mirror.'

'Of course. Lots of times.'

Junipa swung her legs over the edge of the bed and looked at Merle. The mirror-glass eyes blazed golden in the light of the sun rising above the rooftops.

'I don't just mean looked at your reflection.'

'Oh – have I looked behind the surface of the water?'

Junipa nodded. 'Well, have you?'

'Two or three times,' said Merle. 'I dipped my face in as far as I could. The frame's rather a tight fit, but it worked. I got my eyes under water.'

'And?'

'Nothing. Just darkness.'

'You couldn't see anything at all?'

'No, I told you.'

Thoughtfully, Junipa ran her fingers through her hair. 'I'll try if you like.'

Merle, who had been starting to yawn, closed her mouth again. 'You?'

'I can see in the dark with my mirror-glass eyes.'

Merle raised her eyebrows. 'You never told me that.' She suddenly wondered whether she'd done anything to be ashamed of in the night.

'It only started three days ago, but now it's getting clearer every night. I can see as if it was daylight. Sometimes I can't sleep because the brightness comes right through my eyelids. Then everything goes red, as if you were looking straight at the sun with your eyes closed.'

'You'd better tell Arcimboldo about this.'

Junipa looked unhappy. 'But suppose he takes the mirror glass out again?'

'He'd never do that.' Feeling anxious for her friend, Merle tried imagining what it would be like to be surrounded by light all the time, day and night. Suppose it got worse? Would Junipa be able to sleep at all?

'All right,' said Junipa, quickly changing the subject, 'what about it? Shall I try?'

Merle brought the mirror out from under her quilt, felt its weight in her hand for a moment, then shrugged. 'Why not?'

Junipa clambered up on her bed with her. They sat, cross-legged, opposite each other, nightdresses tucked over their knees, both of them with hair still untidy from the night.

'Let me try it myself first,' said Merle.

Junipa watched as Merle brought the mirror very close to her eyes. She cautiously dipped the tip of her nose in, and then – as far as she could – the rest of her face. But the frame soon met her cheekbones. She couldn't get any further in.

She removed the mirror from her face. The water was still all inside the frame; not the slightest trace of moisture showed on her skin.

'Well?' asked Junipa excitedly.

'Nothing.' Merle handed her the mirror. 'Just like before.'

Junipa took the handle in her slim fingers. She looked at the surface of the mirror and studied the reflection of her new eyes. 'Do you think they're pretty?' she asked suddenly.

Merle hesitated. 'Unusual.'

'That's not what I asked.'

'I'm sorry.' Merle wished Junipa could have spared her telling the truth. 'But sometimes I get goosebumps when I look at you. It's not that your eyes are ugly,' she made haste to add. 'They're just so . . . so . . .'

'They feel cold,' said Junipa quietly, as if deep in thought. 'Sometimes I'm freezing, even when the sun shines.'

Brightness by night, cold in the sunshine.

'Will you really do it?' asked Merle.

'I don't particularly want to,' said Junipa. 'But if you think it's a good idea, I'll try for you.' She looked at Merle. 'Or don't you want to know what's behind the mirror where your hand comes out?'

Merle just nodded in silence.

Junipa put her face close to the mirror and then dipped it in. Her head was smaller than Merle's – just as everything about her was more delicate, slender, vulnerable – and so her face went into the water up to the temples.

Merle waited. She watched Junipa's thin body under the nightdress which was much too big for her, saw how her shoulders stuck out under it, while the outline of her collarbones at the neck of her nightie looked as sharp as if they were above her skin instead of under it.

It was a strange, slightly crazy sight to see someone else

reacting to the mirror for the first time. Crazy things can seem quite normal so long as you're doing them yourself, but if you're watching someone else, you wrinkle your nose, turn quickly and go away.

But Merle went on watching, wondering what Junipa was seeing at this moment.

Finally she could stand it no longer, and asked, 'Junipa? Can you hear me?'

Of course she could. Her ears were above the surface of the water. All the same, she didn't answer.

'Junipa?'

Merle felt uneasy, but she didn't do anything yet. Slowly, visions rose in her mind's eye, images of beasts on the other side of the mirror gnawing her friend's face away. In a moment, when she withdrew her head, it would be only a hollow shell of bones and hair, like the helmets of the tribes Professor Burbridge had discovered on his expedition to Hell.

'Junipa?' she asked again, this time a little more sharply. She took the other girl's free hand. Her skin was warm. Merle could feel her pulse.

Junipa returned to her. That was exactly what it was: a return. Her face wore the expression of someone who had been very far away, in distant, unimaginable lands that might have existed on the other side of the world, or only in her imagination.

'What was it?' asked Merle, alarmed. 'What did you see there?'

She would have given a great deal for Junipa to have real human eyes at this moment, eyes in which you could read thoughts. Sometimes you read things there you'd rather not have known, but you always saw the truth.

But Junipa's eyes were shiny and hard and had no movement in them.

Can she still cry? Merle wondered, and the question suddenly seemed more important than anything else.

Junipa did not cry. Only the corners of her mouth twitched. However, it did not look as if she were about to smile.

Merle leaned forward, took the mirror from her hand, put it on the bedspread and took her gently by the shoulders. 'What *is* in the mirror?'

Junipa said nothing for a moment, and then the silvery glass of her eyes turned in Merle's direction. 'It's dark there.'

I know, Merle was going to say, before she realised that

Junipa did not mean the same kind of darkness as she herself had seen.

'Tell me,' she demanded.

Junipa shook her head. 'No. You mustn't ask.'

'What?' exclaimed Merle.

Junipa freed herself from Merle's hands and stood up. 'Never ask me what I saw there,' she said tonelessly. 'Never.'

'But Junipa . . .'

'Please.'

'It can't be anything bad!' cried Merle. Defiance and desperation stirred in her. 'I've felt the hand. The hand, Junipa!'

When a cloud passed over the morning sun outside the window, the brightness of Junipa's mirror-glass eyes dimmed too. 'Let it be, Merle. Forget the hand. It would be a good idea to forget the mirror too.'

And with these words she turned, opened the door and went out into the corridor.

Merle stayed where she was, sitting on the bed, unable to think clearly. Soon she heard a door close, and she felt very much alone.

That day Arcimboldo sent his two girl apprentices hunting mirror phantoms.

'I'm going to show you two something unusual today,' he said that afternoon. Out of the corner of her eye, Merle noticed Dario and the other two boys looking at each other and grinning.

The master mirror-maker pointed to the door leading to the storeroom behind the workshop. 'You have never been in there before,' he said, 'and for good reason.'

Merle had assumed that he feared for the safety of the magic mirrors which were kept there once they had been made.

'Dealing with mirrors such as I make is not without its perils.' Arcimboldo rested both hands on a workbench behind him and leaned back. 'From time to time they must be cleansed of –' he hesitated – 'of certain elements.'

The three boys grinned again. Merle was beginning to feel angry. She hated it when Dario knew more than she did.

'Dario and the others will stay here in the workshop,' said Arcimboldo. 'Junipa and Merle, you two come with me.'

So saying, he turned and went to the storeroom door. Merle and Junipa exchanged glances, then followed him.

'Good luck,' said Boro. It sounded as if he meant it.

'Good luck,' Dario mimicked him, adding something under his breath that Merle didn't catch.

Arcimboldo let the girls in and then closed the door behind them. 'Welcome,' he said, to the heart of my house.'

The sight before them fully justified the solemnity of those words. It was difficult to say how large the room itself was. Its walls were entirely covered with mirrors, and rows of mirrors also ran down the middle of the room, stacked like dominoes about to topple over. Daylight came in through a glass roof – the workshop was in an annexe that was not nearly as tall as the rest of the house.

The mirrors were secured by struts and chains fixed to the walls. Nothing would fall over here unless there was an earthquake in Venice, or unless Hell itself opened up beneath the city – as it was said to have done beneath the North African city of Marrakesh. But that had been over thirty years ago, just after the war broke out. No one mentioned Marrakesh today. It had vanished both from the maps and from conversation.

'How many mirrors are there?' asked Junipa.

It was impossible even to estimate their number, let alone count them. Their glazed surfaces reflected one another over and over again, adding to and multiplying each other. A thought came to Merle: wasn't a mirror that existed only in a mirror just as real as the original? It did its job as well as its real counterpart – it reflected images. Merle could think of nothing else that was able to do something without actually existing itself.

For the first time she wondered whether all mirrors were not really magic mirrors.

Mirrors can see, Arcimboldo had said. She believed him implicitly now.

'You will be meeting some very special kinds of pests,' he told the girls. 'My friends the mirror phantoms.'

'What are the – the mirror phantoms?' Junipa spoke softly, almost reluctantly, as if the images of whatever she had seen behind Merle's water mirror were still before her eyes, frightening her.

Arcimboldo stepped in front of the first mirror in the row down the middle of the room. It reached almost to his chin. Its frame was of plain wood, like the frames of all the mirrors in his workshop. The frames were not for the sake of ornament, but to keep the mirrors from cutting anyone's fingers when they were moved.

'Look carefully,' he said.

The girls went to stand beside him and stared at the

mirror. Junipa was the first to notice it. 'There's something in the glass.'

It looked like wisps of mist drifting very fast across the surface of the mirror, as shapeless as ghosts. And there was no doubt that those pale outlines were *under* the glass and inside the mirror.

'Mirror phantoms,' said Arcimboldo in matter-of-fact tones. 'Irritating parasites that take up residence in my mirrors from time to time. It's the apprentices' job to catch them.'

'How do we do that?' asked Merle.

'You go into the mirrors and get rid of the phantoms with the aid of a little device I'll give you.' He laughed out loud. 'Good heavens, don't look so horrified! Dario and the others have done it any number of times. It may seem a little unusual, but it's not really particularly difficult. Just a nuisance. That's why you apprentices do it while your old master puts his feet up on the table, smokes a good pipe and takes life easy.'

Merle and Junipa exchanged glances. Both of them felt uncertain, but they were determined to acquit themselves well. And anyway, if Dario had done it, so could they.

Arcimboldo took something out of a pocket in his coat.

He held it up between thumb and forefinger in front of the girls' faces. A transparent glass globe no bigger than Merle's clenched fist.

'It doesn't look much, does it?' Arcimboldo smiled, and Merle noticed for the first time that he had a gap in his teeth. 'But it's the best weapon to use against the mirror phantoms. Unfortunately, it's also the only one.'

He fell silent for a moment, but neither girl asked any questions. Merle felt sure that Arcimboldo would explain further.

After a short pause while he gave them an opportunity to look more closely at the glass globe, he said, 'A glass-blower on Murano makes these delightful little things to my designs.'

Designs? Merle wondered. For a plain glass globe?

'If you find yourselves facing a mirror phantom, you have only to say a certain word, and the phantom will instantly be trapped inside the globe,' Arcimboldo told them. 'The word is *intorabiliuspeteris*. You must memorise it as if it were your own name. Intorabiliuspeteris.'

The girls repeated the strange word, stumbling over it once or twice, but then they felt sure they could remember it.

The Master took out a second globe, gave one to each girl, and told them to go up to the mirror. 'Several of my mirrors are infected, but we'll deal with just one today.'

He made a kind of bow in the direction of the mirror and spoke a word in a foreign language.

Then he said, 'Step in.'

'Just like that?' asked Merle.

Arcimboldo laughed. 'Of course. Or would you rather ride in on horseback?'

Merle's glance wandered over the surface of the mirror. It looked smooth and solid, not yielding like the surface of her hand-mirror. The memory of the water mirror made her look briefly at Junipa. Whatever she saw this morning had made a deep impression on her. Now she seemed to be afraid to obey Arcimboldo's instructions. For a moment Merle was tempted to tell the Master everything and ask him to understand, so that Junipa could stay here while she went in alone.

But then Junipa took the first step and put out her hand. Her fingers broke through the surface of the mirror as if it were the skin on a pan of boiled milk. She quickly looked back over her shoulder at Merle, then forced a smile and stepped inside the mirror. She could still be seen, but now she looked flat and somehow unreal, like a figure in a painting. She waved to Merle.

'Brave girl,' murmured Arcimboldo, pleased.

Merle broke through the surface of the mirror with a single step. She felt a cold, tingling sensation, like a breath of wind at midnight, and then she was on the other side and looking round her.

She had once heard rumours of a mirror maze in a palazzo on the Campo Santa Maria Nova. She didn't know anyone who had actually seen it, but the images conjured up in her mind by those rumours didn't for a moment bear comparison with what she saw before her now.

One thing was obvious at first glance: the mirror world was a realm of illusion. It was the space under the false bottom of the conjuror's hat, it was the robbers' cave from the *Thousand and One Nights*, it was the palace of the gods on Mount Olympus. It was artificial, a delusion, a dream that only those who believed in it could dream. Yet at that moment it seemed to Merle as tangible as herself. Did figures in a painting think they were in a real place too? Captives unaware of their captivity?

They were looking at a hall of mirrors. Not like Arcimboldo's storeroom, but a structure consisting of nothing whatsoever but mirrors from top to bottom, from right to left. But this first impression was deceptive: if you took a step forward, you met an invisible glass wall, while where the far end of the hall seemed to be there was nothing but a void, followed by more mirrors, nondescript transit areas, and then yet more illusions.

It took Merle a moment to see what the really confusing thing about this place was: the mirrors reflected only each other, not the two girls standing among them. They could walk straight up to a mirror and bump into it without any warning from their own reflections. This phenomenon continued to infinity on all sides. It was a world of silver and crystal.

Merle and Junipa tried several times to move further into the labyrinth, but again and again they came up against a glassy barrier.

'There's no point in this,' said Merle with annoyance, stamping her foot angrily. The mirror glass crunched under the sole of her shoe, but did not splinter.

'They're all round us,' whispered Junipa.

'The phantoms?'

Junipa nodded.

Merle looked around. 'I can't see any.'

'They're afraid. My eyes scare them. They're flinching away from us.'

Merle turned all the way round. There was a kind of gateway where they had entered the mirror world. She thought she saw movement there, but it was probably only Arcimboldo waiting for them out in the real world.

Something brushed past her face, a pale, flickering thing. Two arms, two legs, a head. At close quarters it no longer looked misty, more like a blur, the result of getting a drop of water in your eye.

Merle raised the glass globe, feeling slightly silly. 'Intorabiliuspeteris,' she said, instantly feeling a great deal sillier.

There was a faint sigh, then the phantom raced towards her. The globe sucked it in. Next moment, the interior of the globe was shimmering and streaky, as if some oily white liquid had been poured into it.

'It works!' exclaimed Merle.

Junipa nodded, but made no move to use her own globe. 'They're very, very frightened now.'

'Can you really see them all round us?'

'Very clearly.'

It must be something to do with Junipa's eyes, with the

magic of the mirror glass. Merle too was now seeing more blurs on the very edge of her field of vision, but her own eyes lacked the clarity to make out the phantoms as Junipa could.

'If they're frightened, that means they're living creatures,' she said, thinking out loud.

'Yes,' said Junipa. 'But it's as if they weren't really here. As if they were just a part of their real selves, like a shadow that's lost the person who cast it.'

'Then perhaps it's a good thing for us to get them out of here. Perhaps they're prisoners.'

'You think they're not prisoners inside the glass globe?'

Junipa was right, of course. But Merle wanted to get out of this glassy maze and back to the real world as quickly as possible. Arcimboldo wouldn't be satisfied unless they caught all the phantoms, and if they didn't she was afraid he would send them straight back into the mirror.

Merle took no more notice of what Junipa was doing. She held out her hand with the globe in it, moved it back and forth, and kept saying the magic word: 'Intorabiliuspeteris . . . Intorabiliuspeteris . . . Intorabiliuspeteris!'

The whispering and rushing grew louder and more distinct, and at the same time the globe filled with that misty turbulence until it looked as if the glass were steamed up on the inside. One of the supervisors at the orphanage had once puffed cigar smoke into a wine glass, and the effect had been very much the same: the streaks twisted and turned behind the glass like a live thing struggling to get out.

What kind of creatures were they, infesting Arcimboldo's magic mirrors like aphids in a vegetable plot? Merle would have loved to know more about them.

Junipa was clutching her globe so tightly in her fist that there was a sudden cracking sound, and it broke in her hand. Tiny splinters rained down on the mirror-glass floor, followed by dark drops of blood as the sharp edges cut Junipa's fingers.

'Junipa!' Merle stuffed her globe in her pocket, ran to Junipa's side and looked at her hand in alarm. 'Oh, Junipa . . .' She slipped her jacket off and wrapped it round her friend's forearm, with the lining next to her skin. As she did so, the upper rim of her hand-mirror showed, sticking out of the other pocket of her dress.

Suddenly one of the phantoms raced around her upper body in a tight spiral and disappeared beneath the surface of the water mirror.

'Oh no!' wept Junipa. 'It's all my fault.'

Merle was more anxious about Junipa than about the mirror. 'I think we've caught them all anyway,' she said between her teeth, unable to take her eyes off the blood on the floor. Her face was reflected in the drops, as if the blood had tiny eyes staring up at her. 'Let's get out of here.'

Junipa held her back. 'Are you going to tell Arcimboldo that one of them got into your –'

'No,' Merle interrupted her. 'He'd only take it away from me.'

Junipa nodded sadly, and Merle put a comforting arm round her shoulders. 'Don't worry about it.'

Gently she guided Junipa back to the gateway, a glittering rectangle not far away from them. Holding each other close, they stepped out of the mirror and back into the storeroom.

'What's happened?' asked Arcimboldo, seeing the wrappings around Junipa's hand. He set to work at once, unwrapped the jacket from around the cuts and hurried to the door. 'Eft!' he shouted into the workshop. 'Bring bandages! Quick!'

Merle too inspected the cuts. Luckily none of them seemed to be really dangerous. Most were not even deep, just red scratches, with thin crusts already coagulating on them.

Junipa pointed to the spots of blood on Merle's crumpled jacket. 'I'll clean it up for you.'

'Eft can do that,' Arcimboldo intervened. 'Tell me what happened.'

Briefly Merle told the story, omitting only the flight of the last phantom into her hand-mirror. 'I caught all the phantoms,' she said, and took the globe out of her pocket. The bright streaks inside it were rotating more violently now.

Arcimboldo took the globe and held it up to the light. What he saw seemed to please him, for he nodded, satisfied. 'You've done well,' he praised the two girls. Not a word about the broken globe.

'Rest now,' he told them after Eft had seen to Junipa's cuts. Then he beckoned to Dario, Boro and Tiziano, who were peering round the storeroom door. 'You three can do the rest.'

As Merle left the workshop with Junipa, she turned back to Arcimboldo again. 'What happens to them now?' She pointed to the globe in the master mirror-maker's hand.

'We throw them into the canal,' he told her, shrugging. 'They can take up residence in the reflections on the water.'

Merle nodded, as if that was what she had expected to hear, and then led Junipa up to their room.

The news went round the workshop like wildfire. There was to be a party! Tomorrow it would be thirty-six years to the day since the armies of the Egyptian Empire reached the shores of the lagoon. Steamships and galleys had cruised on its water, the Barques of the Sun were airborne, ready to attack the defenceless city. But the Flowing Queen had protected Venice, and ever since that day there had been joyful celebrations all over the city on its anniversary. One party was to be held very close to the workshop. Tiziano had heard about it this morning when he went to the fish market with Eft, and he immediately told Dario, who told Boro too, and then, with some reluctance, passed on the news to Merle and Junipa.

'A party in honour of the Flowing Queen! Just round the corner! There'll be paper lanterns hung up everywhere, and beer barrels opened and wine bottles uncorked!'

'And something for you children too?' enquired Arcimboldo, smiling. He had been listening to everything the boys said.

'We're not children any more!' protested Dario, adding

with a sideways glance of derision at Junipa, 'Most of us, anyway.'

Merle was about to leap to Junipa's defence, but it was unnecessary. 'If it shows you're grown up,' said Junipa with unusual sharpness, 'to pick your nose and scratch your bottom in the dark, and do various other things too, then of course you're *very* grown up, aren't you, Dario?'

The boy had gone as red as a turkeycock at her words. Merle too stared at her friend in surprise. Had Junipa slipped into the boys' room by night to see what they were up to? Or could she actually see through walls now with her mirror-glass eyes? The idea made Merle uneasy.

The indignant Dario was ruffled, but Arcimboldo settled the quarrel with a wave of his hand. 'Calm down now, or none of you will go to the party at all! But if you've finished your work by sunset tomorrow, then I see no reason why . . .'

The rest of his words were lost in the apprentices' shouts of delight. Even Junipa's face was beaming. It was as if a shadow had been lifted from her features.

'But there's one thing you should know,' added the master mirror-maker. 'The weaver's apprentices will certainly be there too, and I don't want any trouble. It's bad enough that this canal has become a battle zone, and I won't allow the quarrel to be continued elsewhere. We've drawn enough attention to ourselves as it is. So no insults, no fighting, not even a nasty look at anyone.' His eyes singled Dario out from the others. 'Is that understood?'

Dario took a deep breath, then quickly nodded. The others made haste to mutter their agreement too. At heart, Merle was grateful for Arcimboldo's words, for the last thing she wanted was more brawling with the weaver's boys. Junipa's injuries had done well over the last three days; now they needed rest in order to heal completely.

'All of you back to work, then!' said the Master, satisfied.

To Merle, the time until the party seemed endless. She was excited and could hardly wait to be in company again, not because she was tired of the workshop and the people there – apart from Dario – but she missed the hustle and bustle of life in the streets, the voices of the chattering women, the blatant boasting of the men.

At last the evening came, and the young people left the house together. The boys ran on ahead while Merle and Junipa followed more slowly. Arcimboldo had made Junipa a pair of dark glasses to prevent anyone from noticing her mirror-glass eyes.

The little company turned the corner where the Outcasts' Canal flowed into a wider waterway. Even from a distance they could see hundreds of lights on the facades of the buildings and in the doors and windows. Here the two banks were linked by a narrow bridge, hardly more than a makeshift crossing. Its handrails were adorned with paper lanterns and candles, and people sat on the bridge itself, some on chairs and stools they had brought from their homes, others on cushions or on the bare stone. Drinks were being poured here and there, although, as Merle saw with a certain glee, Dario must have been disappointed; there was hardly any wine and beer, for this was a party for poor people. No one here could afford to spend large sums on grapes or barley that had to be smuggled into the city along perilous routes. The Pharaoh's encircling ring of besiegers was as impenetrable after all these years as at the very beginning of the war. You might not notice it much in everyday life, but no one doubted that hardly a mouse, let alone a smuggler's boat, could slip past the Egyptian army camps. Yes, people could get hold of wine – as Arcimboldo did – but it was usually difficult and even dangerous to do so. The poorer Venetians drank water, and at a party they were content with fruit juice and all kinds of home-made spirits distilled from fruit and vegetables.

Merle saw one of the weaver's apprentices up on the bridge, the boy who had been the first to lose his mask during the scuffle. There were two other lads with him. One of them had a face as red as if it had been sunburnt; obviously he hadn't found it easy to wash off the glue that Merle had squirted inside his mask.

But their leader, Serafin, was nowhere in sight. Merle was surprised to find that, without meaning to, she had been looking out for him and was disappointed not to see him.

Junipa, however, was quite transformed. She couldn't get over her amazement. 'See that man over there?' she kept whispering to Merle, and, 'Oh, do look at that woman!' She chuckled and sometimes laughed so loud that a number of people turned to look at them in surprise, particularly as her dark glasses attracted attention. Only rich and elegant folk who seldom mixed with the common herd usually wore dark glasses. But Junipa's shabby dress left no one in any doubt that she had never seen the inside of a palace.

The two girls stood at the foot of the bridge, on the left-hand side, sipping fruit juice over-diluted with water. A fiddler was playing dance music on the other bank, and soon a flute-player joined him. Young women's skirts spun round and round like brightly coloured tops.

'You take it all so calmly,' said Junipa, hardly knowing where to look first. Merle had never seen her so excited. She was glad, for she had been afraid that all the noise and confusion might frighten Junipa.

'You're looking for that boy.' Junipa's silvery eyes glanced over the top of her glasses. 'Serafin.'

'What makes you think that?'

'I was blind for thirteen years. I know what people are like. If they're sure you can't see, they forget to be cautious. They mix blindness up with deafness. You only have to listen, and they'll tell you all about themselves.'

'So what have I told you about me?' asked Merle, frowning.

Junipa laughed. 'I can see you, and that's quite enough. You keep looking in all directions. So who would you be looking for but Serafin?'

'You're just imagining it.'

'No, I'm not.'

'Yes, you are.'

Junipa's laughter was clear as glass. 'I'm your friend, Merle. Girls do *talk* about that kind of thing.'

Merle pretended to hit out at her, and Junipa giggled like a child.

'Oh, leave me alone!' cried Merle, laughing.

Junipa looked up. 'There he is.'

'Where?'

'There, over on the other side.'

Junipa was right. Serafin was sitting a little to one side, on the edge of the paved path, dangling his legs over the canal. The soles of his feet were dangerously close to the water.

'Go over to him,' said Junipa.

'No, never!'

'Why not?'

'Well, he's a weaver's apprentice. One of our enemies, remember? I can't just . . . I mean, it wouldn't be proper.'

'It'd be even less proper to pretend you're listening to me when your real thoughts are somewhere else entirely.'

'Can you read thoughts with your new eyes too?' asked Merle, amused.

Junipa shook her head in all seriousness, as if she really had considered that possibility. 'I only have to look at you.'

'You really think I ought to go over and speak to him?'

'You bet I do.' Junipa grinned. 'Or are you scared?'

'Nonsense. I only want to ask him how long he's been working for Umberto,' Merle said defensively.

'What a *terrible* excuse!'

'You silly goose! No – no, you're not. You're a darling!' Merle flung her arms around Junipa, hugged her briefly, and then ran over the bridge to the opposite bank. On her way she looked back over her shoulder and saw Junipa watching her with a slight smile.

'Hi.'

Merle stopped, surprised. Serafin must have seen her coming, because all of a sudden there he was, right in front of her.

'Hi,' she said, sounding as if she had just swallowed a plum stone. 'So you're here too?'

'Looks like it.'

'I thought you might prefer to stay at home. Thinking up plans for throwing paint bombs in other people's faces.'

'Oh, that . . .!' He grinned. 'We don't do it every day. Would you like something to drink?'

She had left her mug behind with Junipa, so she nodded. 'Juice, please.'

Serafin turned and went over to a fruit-juice stall. Merle

watched his back view. He was a little taller than she was, rather thin, perhaps, but then they all were. People born in a city under siege don't have to worry about their weight. Unless, she thought cynically, your name is Ruggero and you eat half the food in the orphanage larder on the sly.

Serafin came back and handed her a wooden mug. 'Apple juice,' he said. 'I hope you like it.'

For the sake of politeness she sipped some at once. 'Yes, very much.'

'You're new at Arcimboldo's, aren't you?'

'You know I am.' She immediately regretted her words. Why snap at him like that? Couldn't she just talk to him normally? 'Yes, I've been there a few weeks now,' she added.

'Were you and your friend in the same orphanage before?'

She shook her head. 'No.'

'Arcimboldo's done something to her eyes.'

'Junipa was blind. She can see again now.'

'Then what Master Umberto says is right.'

'What does he say?'

'He says Arcimboldo can work magic.'

'Other people say the same about Umberto.'

Serafin grinned. 'I've been in his house for over two years and he's never shown me a single magic trick.'

'I guess Arcimboldo will keep that to the very last, too.'

They laughed a little nervously, not because they'd found something in common for the first time, but because neither of them knew just how to continue the conversation.

'Shall we go for a walk?' Serafin pointed down the canal to where there were no crowds of people, and the lanterns shone down on empty water.

Merle smiled mischievously. 'A good thing we're not in high society, or that wouldn't be proper, would it?'

'I don't care a bit about high society.'

'Something else we have in common.'

Close together, but not quite touching, they walked along the canal. The music faded and soon died away behind them. Water lapped rhythmically against the dark walls. Somewhere up above, pigeons cooed in the niches and stucco ornamentation of the buildings. They turned a corner and found themselves away from the light of all the lanterns.

'Have you had to chase the ghosts out of the mirrors yet?' asked Serafin after a while.

'Ghosts? Do you think those phantom shapes haunting the mirrors are real ghosts?'

'Master Umberto says they're the ghosts of all the people Arcimboldo has taken for a ride.'

Merle laughed. 'And you believe him?'

'No,' said Serafin gravely. 'Because I know better.'

'But you're a weaver, not a mirror-maker.'

'I've only been a weaver for two years. Before that, I was chasing around all over Venice.'

'Do you have parents?'

'Not as far as I know. At least, they've never turned up to introduce themselves.'

'But you weren't in an orphanage.'

'No, I lived in the streets. Like I said, all over the place. And I picked up all kinds of things then, too. Things not everybody knows.'

'Like how to gut a rat before you eat it?' she asked mockingly.

He made a face at her. 'That too, yes. But it wasn't what I meant.'

A black cat brushed past them, then turned and came back. Without warning, it jumped up at Serafin, but not to attack him. Instead it landed on his shoulder and sat there, purring. Serafin didn't even start in surprise, just lifted a hand and began stroking the animal.

'You're a thief!' exclaimed Merle. 'Only thieves are such friends with cats.'

'Vagabonds, the lot of us!' he agreed, smiling. 'Thieves and cats do have a lot in common. And they share a lot too.' He sighed. 'But yes, you're right. I grew up among thieves. I was a member of the Guild when I was five, and later I became a Master.'

'A Master Thief!' Merle was amazed. The Masters of the Guild of Thieves were the most skilful pickpockets in Venice. 'But you can't be more than fifteen!'

He nodded. 'I left the Guild when I was thirteen and entered Umberto's service. He needed someone like me – someone to climb quietly in through ladies' windows by night delivering the goods they ordered. You probably know that most husbands aren't too happy for their wives to buy from Umberto. His reputation is –'

'Bad?'

'Well, kind of. But his dresses make women look thin, and most wives don't want their husbands to know how much plumper they really are. Umberto's reputation may not be very good, but his business is doing better than ever.'

'But the men will find out the truth when their wives . . .' Merle's cheeks flushed red. 'Well, when they get undressed. At the latest.'

'Oh, there are ways of getting round that. They put out the light, or they make sure their husbands have had a few drinks. Women are cleverer than you might think.'

'I *am* a woman!'

'In a couple of years, maybe.'

She stopped, indignantly. 'Serafin the Master Thief, I don't think you know enough about women – apart from where they keep their purses – to say a thing like that.'

The black cat on Serafin's shoulder hissed at Merle, but she took no notice.

Serafin whispered something in the cat's ear, and it calmed down immediately.

'I didn't mean to insult you.' He genuinely did look upset by Merle's spat of temper. 'Really I didn't.'

She looked hard at him. 'All right, then I'll forgive you this time.'

He bowed, so that the cat had to dig its claws into his shirt. 'My humblest thanks, gracious lady.'

Merle hastily looked away so that he wouldn't see her laughing. When she glanced back at him, the cat had gone. There were bright red spots of blood on the fabric of his shirt, where its claws had dug into his shoulder.

'That must hurt,' she said with concern.

'Which hurts more, the claws of a cat or a prickly woman?'

She decided not to answer that one. Instead she walked on, and Serafin was beside her again at once.

'You were going to tell me something else about the mirror phantoms,' she said.

'Was I?'

'Well, you shouldn't have started if you weren't going to go on.'

Serafin nodded. 'You're right. It's just –' He suddenly fell silent, stopped, and listened to the night.

'What is it?'

'Ssh,' he said, gently laying a finger on her lips.

She listened intently in the darkness. You heard some very strange noises in the alleys and waterways of Venice, where the narrow space between the buildings could distort sound until it was unrecognisable. In the dark, the winding labyrinth of alleys seemed deserted, for most people preferred the livelier main thoroughfares at this time of night. Robbers and assassins made many parts of the city unsafe, and sometimes the sounds of screams, sobs or violent blows heard by the old walls were carried, as echoes, to places far from their origin. If Serafin really had heard an alarming noise, it might mean anything or nothing: the danger could be round the next corner or hundreds of metres away.

'Soldiers!' he whispered, seizing the startled Merle by the arm and pulling her into one of the narrow tunnels that ran under many buildings in the city: roofed alleys that were pitch dark by night.

'Are you sure?' she whispered, close to his cheek, and felt him nod.

'Two men mounted on lions. Round the corner.'

Then she saw the two of them, uniformed men with swords and guns riding grey basalt lions. With their majestic tread, the great cats carried their riders past the mouth of the tunnel, moving with astonishing grace. Their bodies were massive stone, yet they stepped as delicately as agile domestic cats. Their claws, as sharp as dagger blades, scraped over the paved road surface, leaving deep furrows behind.

When the patrol was far enough away, Serafin whispered, 'Quite a number of them know my face. I'm not too keen to meet them.'

'I'm sure that's sensible, for someone who was a Master Thief at thirteen.'

He smiled, flattered. 'Could be!'

'Why did you leave the Guild?'

'The older masters didn't like it when I came back with richer pickings than they did. They spread lies about me and tried to get me thrown out of the Guild. So I thought it better to go of my own accord.' He stepped out of the tunnel into the soft light of a gas lamp. 'Well, come on – I promised to tell you more about the ghosts in the mirrors, but there's something I have to show you first.'

They walked on through the maze of narrow alleys and passages, turning right here, left there, crossing bridges over quiet canals, passing through gateways and under the washing lines slung between buildings like a parade of pale, ghostly sheets. They met not a single human being on their way, another feature of this strangest of all cities: you could often walk kilometres without seeing a soul, just cats and rats hunting among the rubbish.

The alley ahead of them ended beside a canal. No paths ran along its bank; the walls of the houses went straight down into the water, and there was no bridge anywhere to be seen.

'A blind alley,' murmured Merle 'We'll have to turn back.'

Serafin shook his head. 'This is where I meant to go.' He

leaned a little way over the side of the canal and glanced up at the sky, a black streak running between the buildings. Then he looked across the water. 'See that?'

Merle joined him. Her eyes followed his pointing finger to the gently rippling surface of the canal. The brackish smell of the water rose to her nostrils, but she hardly noticed. Trailing seaweed drifted in the canal, much more of it than usual.

A lighted window, the only one anywhere near, was reflected in the water. It was in the second storey of a house on the other side of the canal. The opposite bank was about five metres away.

'I don't know what you mean,' she said.

'Do you see the light in that window?'

'Of course.'

Serafin took out a silver pocket-watch, an expensive piece, probably dating from the days of his career as a thief. He snapped the lid open. 'Ten minutes past twelve. We're on the dot.'

'So?'

He grinned. 'I'll explain. You see the reflection on the water, right?'

She nodded.

'Good. Then look up at the building and show me the window that's reflected in the canal. The one with the light behind it.'

Merle looked up at the sombre facade. All the windows were dark. Not a single one had any light in it. She looked down at the water again. The reflection was still the same: light was burning in one of the windows reflected in the water. When she looked up at the building once more, the rectangle in the wall was still dark.

'How can that be?' she asked, confused. 'There's light in the reflection of the window, but the real window is perfectly dark.'

Serafin's grin grew even broader. 'So it is.'

'Magic?'

'Not entirely. Or maybe it is, depending on how you look at it.'

She frowned. 'Could you explain yourself a little more clearly?'

'It always happens during the hour after midnight. Between twelve and one in the morning. You can see the same phenomenon at several places in the city. Not many people know about it, and a number of those places I haven't seen myself, but it's a fact: during that hour a few buildings in Venice cast a reflection on the water that doesn't match reality. There are only tiny differences. Lights in windows, sometimes an extra door, people walking past buildings when there's no one really there.'

'But what does it mean?'

'No one knows for sure. But there are rumours.' He lowered his voice, sounding very mysterious. 'Tales of a *second* Venice.'

'A second Venice?'

'One that exists only in the reflection on the water. Or at least, one so far away from ours that you couldn't reach it in the fastest of ships. Not even in the Empire's Barques of the Sun. They say it's in another world, a world like ours but at the same time quite different. And at midnight the border between the two cities leaks, perhaps just because it's so old that it's worn thin over the centuries, like a tattered carpet.'

Merle looked at him, wide-eyed. 'You mean that window with the light in it – you're saying it really does exist, but not *here*?'

'And listen to this. An old beggar who's had his pitch close to one of these places for years, observing it day and night, told me more. He says men and women from that other Venice sometimes manage to pass through the barrier between the worlds. What they don't know is that, once they arrive here, they're not real human beings any more, only phantoms caught for ever in the city's reflections. Some of them manage to leap from mirror to mirror, so now and then they stray into your master's workshop and into his magic mirrors.'

Merle wondered if Serafin was teasing her. 'You're not trying to pull my leg, are you?'

Serafin grinned, showing his teeth. 'Do I look as if I could tell anyone a fib?'

'Oh, not for a moment, most noble Master Thief.'

'Well, anyway, that's how I heard the story. I can't tell you how much of it is true.' He pointed to the lighted window in the water. 'There does seem to be some evidence in favour of it, though.'

'But then I was imprisoning real people in that glass globe today!'

'Don't worry. I've seen Arcimboldo throw the globes into the canal. The phantoms must manage to get out again somehow.'

'And now I see what he meant when he said they could take up residence in the reflections on the water.' She took a deep breath. 'Arcimboldo knows! He knows the truth!'

'What are you going to do? Ask him about it?'

She shrugged. 'Why not?' But she did not pursue the idea further, for suddenly there was movement on the water. When she looked more closely, she saw a shape gliding over the surface of the canal towards them.

'Is that –?' She broke off when she realised that this reflection was no illusion.

'Get back!'

Serafin had seen it too. They darted back into the alley and pressed close to the wall.

Something large was approaching from the left, flying just above the water without touching it. It was a lion with mighty wings; like its whole body, the plumage of those wings was made of stone. The wing tips almost touched the walls of the buildings on both sides of the canal. The lion flew almost soundlessly; only the leisurely beating of its wings made a faint murmur like the sound of breathing. The wind of its passing blew cold in Merle and Serafin's faces. The enormous mass and weight of the lion's body was deceptive; it hovered in the air as lightly as a bird. It held its forepaws and hind paws at an angle, and its mouth was tightly closed. Its sparkling eyes showed bewildering intelligence, far keener than the minds of ordinary animals.

The severe figure of a soldier sat on the lion's back. His uniform was of black leather reinforced with steel rivets. One of the councillors' bodyguards, a man whose task it was to provide one of the great lords with personal protection. You seldom met these guards, and if you did it generally boded no good.

The lion and its rider flew past the mouth of the alley without noticing the two young people. Merle and Serafin dared not breathe until the great cat, flying on, had left them far behind. Then they cautiously leaned forward and saw the lion gain height, leave the narrow shaft of the canal, and begin to describe a wide loop in the air above the rooftops of the quarter. Soon they lost sight of it.

'It's circling,' said Serafin. 'Whoever it's protecting can't be far off.'

'A city councillor?' whispered Merle. 'At this time of night and in this part of town? Never! They don't leave their palaces unless they absolutely must.'

'There aren't many flying lions. Those few that are left never go further than necessary from their masters.' Serafin took a deep breath. 'So one of the councillors must be very close.'

As if to underline his words, the roar of a flying lion

echoed in the darkness of the night sky. A second lion answered the call. And then a third.

'Several of them.' Merle shook her head, puzzled. 'What are they doing here?'

Serafin's eyes shone. 'We could find out.'

'How about the lions, though?'

'I've often got away from flying lions.'

Merle wasn't sure whether he was boasting or telling the truth. Maybe both. She didn't know him well enough to make up her mind. Her instinct told her that she could trust him. *Must* trust him – or so it seemed at the moment – for Serafin had already set off for the other end of the alley.

She hurried after him until they were level again. 'I hate having to run after other people.'

'It's sometimes a good idea to make quick decisions.'

She snorted. 'And I hate it even more when other people want to make my decisions for me.'

He stopped and drew her back by the arm. 'You're right. This is something we must both really *want* to do, because it could get quite dangerous.'

Merle sighed. 'I'm not the sort of girl who gives up easily – so don't treat me like one. And I'm not afraid of flying lions either.' Well, of course not, she added to herself. I've never been chased by one so far.

'No reason to be so huffy.'

'I'm not.'

'Yes, you are.'

'And you're always trying to pick a quarrel.'

He grinned. 'An occupational disease.'

'Show-off! You're not a thief any more.' She walked away from him. 'Come on, or there won't be any lions or councillors or adventures at all for us tonight.'

This time it was he who followed her. She had a feeling that he was putting her to the test. Would she go in the same direction as the one he had chosen? Was she interpreting the distant wingbeats in the sky correctly, letting them lead her to the right destination?

She'd show Serafin a thing or two!

She hurried round more corners, still looking up from time to time at the night sky beyond the edges of the rooftops, before she finally slowed down, trying to make no sound at all. From now on they were in danger of discovery. But she didn't know whether that danger threatened to come down from the sky or out of the entrance of some building.

'It's the house over there,' whispered Serafin.

Her gaze followed his pointing finger to the doorway of a narrow building with a facade just wide enough for the door and two barred windows. It looked as if it had once been the servants' quarters of a grand palazzo somewhere nearby, at a time when the facades of Venice still proclaimed the splendour and riches of their owners. But today the palaces were as empty as most of the houses along the Outcasts' Canal and everywhere else. Even vagabonds and beggars wouldn't live there, for it was impossible to heat those huge halls in winter. Firewood had been in short supply since the beginning of the siege, and long ago people had begun gutting the city's abandoned buildings, tearing out their rafters and panelled ceilings to burn in the cold months of the year.

'Why that house in particular?' asked Merle softly.

Serafin pointed to the roof. Merle had to admit that he possessed remarkably keen eyesight. Something showed over the edge of the roof: a stone claw clamped round a tile. From the street you couldn't see the lion on guard up there in the darkness. All the same, Merle did not doubt for a moment that watchful eyes were staring down from the dark roof.

She and Serafin were standing in the shadow of a house

entrance, invisible from above, but if they came out and ran to the narrow building, the watcher on the roof would be sure to see them.

'Let's try the back way,' Serafin suggested in a quiet voice.

'But the back of the building goes straight down to the canal!' Merle's sense of direction in these narrow alleys was infallible. She knew exactly what it would be like behind this row of houses, where the walls fell smooth and vertical, and there was no path along the canal bank.

'We can do it all the same,' said Serafin. 'Trust me.'

'As a friend or a master thief?'

He paused for a moment, put his head on one side and looked at her in surprise. Then he put out his hand. 'Friends?' he asked tentatively.

She took his hand firmly in hers. 'Friends.'

Serafin gave her a wide, beaming grin. 'Then as a master thief I can assure you we'll get into that building somehow or other. And as a friend . . .' He hesitated briefly and then began again. 'As a friend I promise I'll never let you down, whatever happens tonight.'

He did not wait for an answer, but drew her back with him into the shadows of the alley out of which they had come. They made straight for their destination, through the tunnel, over a back yard and past several empty buildings.

It seemed to be no time before they were making their way along a narrow ledge which ran along the back of a row of houses. The water rocked below them, black as night. The arch of a bridge could be vaguely seen in the darkness, twenty metres away. A lion with an armed rider stood on the highest point of the bridge. The man had his back turned to them. Even if he did look behind him, he would have difficulty spotting them in the dark.

'Let's hope the lion doesn't pick up our scent,' whispered Merle. Like Serafin, she was pressing close to the wall. The ledge was just wide enough to take her heels. She had difficulty keeping her balance and at the same time watching the guard posted on the bridge.

The ledge presented Serafin with fewer problems. He was used to gaining unconventional entry into strange buildings, first as a thief and then as Umberto's secret messenger. All the same, he didn't make Merle feel that she was holding him up.

'Why doesn't he turn round?' he whispered between gritted teeth. 'I don't like it.'

Being a little shorter than Serafin, Merle could see rather further along the canal when she peered under the bridge.

And now she saw a boat approaching from the opposite direction. She told Serafin about her discovery in a whisper. 'It doesn't seem to bother the guard. Looks as if he was expecting the boat.'

'A secret assignation,' Serafin guessed. 'I've known that to happen several times before. A councillor meeting one of his informants. They say the City Council has its spies everywhere, and in every class of the population.'

Merle had worries of a very different kind just at the moment. 'How much further?'

Serafin leaned very slightly forward. 'About three metres, then we'll reach the first window. If it's open, we can climb into the house.' He looked round at Merle. 'Can you see who's in the boat?'

She stared as hard as she could, hoping to make out the figure standing upright in the bows more clearly. But like the two oarsmen sitting further back, it was wrapped in a black, hooded cloak. Not surprising, considering the time of night and the cold air, yet Merle shivered at the sight. Was she mistaken, or was the lion up on the bridge scraping one paw nervously on the paved surface?

Serafin reached the window. They were less than ten metres from the bridge now. He peered cautiously through the glass, then nodded to Merle. 'The room's empty. They must be in another part of the house.'

'Can you open the window?' Merle did not mind heights particularly, but her back was beginning to hurt, and a numb, tingling sensation was creeping up her tense legs.

Serafin pressed the glass, first gently, then a little more forcefully. There was a soft, cracking sound. The right-hand side of the window swung inwards.

Merle breathed a sigh of relief. Thank goodness! She tried to keep her eye on the boat while Serafin clambered into the house. The boat had tied up on the other side of the bridge. The lion carried its rider down to the bank of the canal to receive the hooded figure.

Merle saw the flying lions in the sky. At least three of them, perhaps more. If one of them came down again and flew along the canal, it would be sure to see her.

But Serafin was already putting his hand out to her through the window, pulling her inside the house. With another huge sigh, she felt wooden planks beneath her feet. She was so relieved, she could have kissed those planks. Or Serafin. No, better not.

'You're all red,' he commented.

'I was making an effort!' she quickly rejoined, turning her face away. 'So now what?'

He took his time before answering. At first she thought he was still staring at her, perhaps to decide whether the effort she'd been making was really the reason for her red cheeks; then she realised that he was listening, just as Junipa had listened during their journey to the Outcasts' Canal. Concentrating intently, so that not the faintest sound would escape him.

'They're at the front of the house again,' he said at last. 'Two men at least, perhaps three.'

'With the soldiers, that makes about half a dozen.'

'Afraid?'

'Not a bit.'

He smiled. 'Now who's showing off?'

She couldn't help answering his smile. He saw through her even in the dark. With anyone else she'd have felt uncomfortable about that. But he had said, 'Trust me,' and she found that she did. Everything was going much too fast, but she didn't have time to let that bother her.

Quiet as mice, they stole out of the room and made their way along a dark passage. The front door of the building lay at the end of it. There was a glow of candlelight in the first corridor on their right. On their left, a flight of stairs led up to the first floor.

Serafin put his lips very close to Merle's ear. 'Wait here. I'll take a look round.'

She was about to protest, but he quickly shook his head.

'Please,' he added.

She felt anxious as she watched him move silently along the lighted corridor. The front door might open at any moment and let in the man wearing the hooded cloak, accompanied by the soldier.

Serafin reached the door, he looked cautiously through the crack where it stood ajar, paused briefly and then came back to Merle. Silently he pointed to the steps going up.

Without a sound, she followed his directions. He, not she, was the master thief. He presumably knew the best thing to do, even if she found it difficult to admit as much. She didn't like doing as other people told her. Even when it was in her own best interests.

The stairs were of solid stone. Merle went ahead and, once they were on the first floor, turned towards the room above the candlelit room on the ground floor. When they got there, she realised what had sent Serafin upstairs.

About one-third of the floor of this upper room had

collapsed long ago. Splintered wooden planks stood out from the edges of a large hole in the middle of the room, framing it. Candlelight shone up from below. Muted voices could be heard. They sounded uncertain and intimidated, although Merle couldn't make out the exact words.

'Three men,' Serafin whispered in her ear. 'All of them councillors. Great lords.'

Merle peered over the edge of the gap. She could feel the warmth of the candlelight rising to her face. Serafin was right. The three men standing side by side down there wore the long robes of members of the Council, one in gold, one in purple, one in scarlet.

There was no higher authority in all Venice than the Council. Since the invasion of the Egyptian Empire, when all contact with the mainland had been broken, they had wielded authority over the affairs of the besieged city. They held all power in their hands, and they kept in contact with the Flowing Queen – or at least, so they said. Outwardly they appeared sophisticated and infallible. But there were certain rumours complaining of their abuse of power, of nepotism, of the decadence of the old, noble families to which most members of the Council belonged. The rich took precedence, that was no secret. If you could show that yours was an ancient family name, you were worth more than the common herd.

One of the three men in the ground-floor room was holding a wooden casket in his hands. It looked like an ebony jewellery box.

'What are they doing here?' Merle's lips formed the question without uttering a sound.

Serafin shrugged his shoulders.

There was a creaking noise down in the hall as the front door was opened. Footsteps were heard, and then a soldier's voice.

'My lords,' the soldier announced obsequiously, 'the Egyptian envoy has arrived.'

'Hold your tongue, for heaven's sake!' hissed the councillor in the purple robe. 'Do you want the whole quarter to know?'

The soldier turned and left the house as his companion entered the room. He was the man from the boat, and he still wore his hood pulled well forward to hide his face. The candlelight was not bright enough to show the shadowed features under it.

He did not trouble with any greeting. 'Have you brought what you promised?'

Merle had never heard an Egyptian voice before. She was surprised to find that the man spoke without any foreign accent at all, but she was too tense with apprehension to realise the implications at once. Only gradually did their monstrous significance dawn on her. A secret meeting between members of the City Council and an Egyptian envoy! Presumably a spy, living in disguise in the city itself, or his Venetian accent wouldn't be so perfect.

Serafin was as white as a sheet. Perspiration stood out on his forehead. Badly shaken, he looked over the edge of the hole in the floor and down to the room below.

The councillor in gold sketched a bow, and the two others followed his lead. 'We are glad you have agreed to our request for a meeting. And yes, we have what you want with us.'

The councillor in scarlet nervously twined his fingers together. 'No doubt the Pharaoh will prove grateful?'

The black opening in the hood was abruptly turned towards the last speaker. 'The God-Emperor Amenophis will be told of your request for an alliance with us. What happens then is in his divine hands alone.'

'Of course, of course.' The councillor in purple made haste to mollify the Egyptian. He cast an angry glance at the man in the scarlet robe. 'We do not mean to question any decision made by his Divinity.'

'Where is it?'

The councillor in gold held the casket out to the envoy. 'With our most humble greetings to Pharaoh Amenophis. From his faithful servants.'

Traitor, thought Merle with contempt. *Traitor, traitor, traitor!* The grovelling tone adopted by the three city councillors made her feel quite ill. Or was it just fear turning her stomach?

The envoy took the casket and opened the catch. The councillors exchanged uncertain glances.

Merle leaned further forward to get a better view of the interior of the casket. Serafin too was craning his head to see more.

The casket was lined with velvet, and on it lay a little crystal flask no longer than a finger. The envoy carefully took it out and tossed the box aside. It fell to the floor with a crash. The noise made the councillors jump.

Taking the flask between thumb and forefinger, the man raised it to the level of his hooded face, holding it up to the candlelight.

'At last, after all these years!' he murmured, lost in thought.

Puzzled, Merle looked at Serafin. What was so valuable about that tiny flask?

The councillor in purple raised his hands in a solemn gesture. 'It really is in there – the essence of the Flowing Queen. The magic you made available to us has worked a true miracle.'

Merle held her breath as she exchanged glances of alarm with Serafin.

'The Pharaoh's alchemists spent twice ten years developing the method,' said the envoy coolly. 'There was never any doubt that the magic would work.'

'Of course not, of course not.'

The councillor in scarlet, who had been looking awkward enough already, shifted from foot to foot in his agitation. 'But all your magic wouldn't have helped you if we hadn't agreed to cast the spells in the presence of the Flowing Queen. No servant of the Pharaoh would ever have come so close to her.'

The envoy's tone of voice was ominous. 'Then do I understand that you are *not* a servant of the Pharaoh, Councillor de Angeliis?'

The councillor addressed turned as white as a sheet. 'Of course I am, of course, of course.'

'You are nothing but a miserable coward. And one of the worst sort: a traitor!'

The councillor looked down his nose defiantly. He shook off the hand that the councillor in purple, trying to pacify him, laid on his arm. 'Without us you'd never –'

'Councillor de Angeliis!' snapped the envoy, and now his voice rose like an angry old woman's. 'You'll get the reward for your services, if that's what you're worried about. You will get it, at the latest, when the Pharaoh and his armies enter the lagoon and confirm the three of you in office as his administrators. But now, in the name of Amenophis, kindly keep quiet!'

'If you will permit me to say so,' said the councillor in purple, ignoring de Angeliis, whose face was a pitiful sight, 'you should know that time is pressing. An envoy from Hell has once again announced his forthcoming visit to offer us a pact against the Empire. I don't know how long we three shall be able to oppose the idea. Other members of the council are more receptive to this offer from Hell. We can't keep them in check for ever. Particularly as the envoy has said that on the occasion of his next visit he will appear in public, so that even the common people will hear of his request.'

The envoy let out his breath with a hissing sound. 'That must not happen. The attack on the lagoon is imminent. A pact with Hell could ruin everything.' He paused briefly to think the situation over. 'If this envoy does appear, make sure that he has no chance to appeal to the people. Kill him!'

'But the vengeance of Hell –' de Angeliis began in a subdued voice.

However, the third councillor silenced him with a gesture.

'Of course, lord,' said the councillor in gold, bowing towards the envoy. 'It shall be done as you say. The Empire will protect us from any consequences once it has the city under its control.'

The Egyptian nodded graciously. 'So be it.'

Merle's lungs were crying out for air. She couldn't hold her breath a second longer. The sound as she drew in air was faint, hardly audible, yet loud enough to attract the attention of the councillor in scarlet. He looked up at the hole in the ceiling. Merle and Serafin were just in time to withdraw their heads. They heard the rest of what the envoy was saying, but they couldn't see what was going on down below.

'The desert crystal of which that flask is made is strong enough to hold the Flowing Queen captive. Her rule over the lagoon is ended. An army of many thousand warriors stands ready on land and on the water. As soon as the Pharaoh has this flask in his hands, the galleys and the Barques of the Sun will strike.'

Merle felt a movement at her right side. She looked round, but Serafin was too far away for it to be him. And yet – something was certainly moving at her hip! A rat? She realised the truth only when it was too late.

Like a living thing, the water mirror had slipped out of the pocket of her dress. It was making the jerky, clumsy movements of a blinded animal. Then everything happened very fast. Merle tried to grab the mirror, but it shot away from under her hand, slid towards the edge of the hole in the floor, toppled over it – and fell.

In a long, long moment that might have been frozen in time, Merle saw that the surface of the mirror, clouded by the presence of the phantom, had turned milky white.

The mirror dropped to the depths below, where Merle's outstretched hand could not catch it, fell straight towards the envoy, missed his hood, struck his hand, and knocked the crystal flask out of his fingers. The man screamed with pain, with anger, with surprise, while mirror and flask crashed to the floor at almost the same time.

'*No!*' Serafin's cry made the three councillors spring apart, scattering like drops of hot fat. With a bold leap, he swung himself over the edge of the hole and landed among them. Merle had no time to stop and think about this sudden disastrous development. Her dress ballooned out in the air as she followed Serafin down, uttering a loud yell which she meant to be very fierce, although it probably sounded anything but.

The envoy flinched back, or her feet would have struck his head. He swiftly bent and tried to pick up the crystal flask. But his hand missed it and instead touched the water mirror. For a fraction of a second his fingertips dipped below its surface, disappeared right in it – and when the envoy withdrew his hand with a cry of pain they were gone. Instead, blackened splinters of bone now emerged from the ends of his fingers, charred and smoking as if he had put his hand into a barrel of acid.

A wild screech came from under the hood. Uttered by no visible face or mouth, it sounded inhuman.

Putting both hands to the floor, Serafin turned a cart-wheel almost faster than the eye could see. When he came to rest on his feet again beside the window, he was holding the flask in his right hand and Merle's mirror in his left hand.

Meanwhile the councillor in purple, spokesman for the traitors, had seized Merle's upper arm and was trying to pull her round to face him. Fist clenched, he was about to strike her, while the other two councillors ran around like frightened chickens, shouting for their bodyguards. Quick as lightning, Merle swerved and managed to shake off the hand on her arm, but as she did so her back came up against black fabric. The envoy's robe. A stench of burned flesh surrounded him.

Keen air whistled through the gaps in the boards over the window: flying lions were landing outside the house. Steel scraped on steel as swords were drawn from their scabbards.

An arm came around Merle from behind, but she ducked under it, as she used to in so many brawls in the orphanage. She had experience of fighting, and she knew where to hit to make it hurt. As Councillor de Angeliis barred her way, she placed a well-aimed kick. The fat man in the scarlet robe yelled blue murder and clutched his lower body with both hands.

'Out of here!' cried Serafin, holding off the other two councillors by threatening to smash the flask on the floor – regardless of the consequences.

Merle raced towards him and ran to the door of the room

with him. They reached the hall at the very moment when the front door was pushed open and two bodyguards clad in black leather came clattering in.

'By the Traitor of Old!' Serafin swore.

The soldiers stopped, taken aback. They had been expecting some Egyptian trick, men armed to the teeth, opponents worthy of two battle-hardened guardsmen. Instead they saw a girl in a shabby dress and a boy holding in his hands two shining objects which did not look at all like blades.

Merle and Serafin took advantage of that moment of surprise. Before the guards could react, they were both on their way to the back room.

But there, by the open window, the envoy was waiting. He had known there was only one way of escape for them – out of the back of the house, into the water.

'The mirror!' Merle called to Serafin.

He threw it to her, and she caught it in both hands and struck out at the envoy with it. He swerved nimbly, but that left her way to the window free. His singed fingertips were still smoking.

'The flask!' he demanded hoarsely. 'You are defying the Pharaoh!'

Serafin uttered a reckless laugh that surprised even Merle. Then he took off from a standing position and performed a rolling leap through the air. It took him past the envoy and the hands trying to seize him. He landed safely in the window frame and perched there like a bird, sitting with both feet on the frame, his knees drawn up and a broad grin on his face.

'All honour to the Flowing Queen!' he cried, as Merle used the moment to jump up beside him. 'Follow me!'

So saying, he let himself drop backwards out of the window and down to the still water of the canal.

It was not so much his hand that swept Merle away with him as his spirit, his sheer determination not to give up. For the first time in her life she felt true admiration for another human being.

The envoy screamed and managed to seize the hem of Merle's dress, but he caught it with the fingers of his seared hand and immediately let go again, bellowing like an ox.

The water was icy. Within the space of a single heartbeat it seemed to penetrate their clothes, their flesh, their whole bodies. Merle couldn't breathe, couldn't move, couldn't even think. Afterwards, she had no idea how long this state lasted, though it felt like several minutes, but then she came up to the surface, Serafin was beside her, and life came back into her limbs. She couldn't have been underwater for more than a second or so at the most.

'Here, take this!' Beneath the surface, he pressed the flask into her left hand. Her right hand still held the mirror, which lay between her fingers as if welded to them.

'What do you want me to do with it?'

'If the worst comes to the worst, I'll draw their attention away from you,' said Serafin, spitting out water. The ripples were breaking against his lips.

If the worst comes to the worst? thought Merle. Even worse than this?

The envoy appeared at the window, shouting something.

Serafin whistled. He succeeded only at the second attempt; his first try brought only water spurting from his lips. Following his eyes to the window, Merle saw black shapes scurrying down from above, four-legged shadows leaping out of nooks and crannies, niches and gutters, screeching and mewing, claws out to dig into the envoy's cloak. One cat landed on the window sill, took off again and disappeared entirely inside the darkness of the hood. The Egyptian staggered back into the room, screaming.

'A harmless thieves' trick!' said Serafin, pleased with himself.

'We must get out of the water and back to land!' Merle turned and let the mirror slip into the pocket of her dress, together with the flask. She was wasting no more thought on that just now. She started swimming, taking a few strokes towards the opposite bank. The walls there came right down into the canal, and there were no handholds to help them scramble up on to dry land. Never mind, they had to do something.

'Back to land?' Serafin, echoed, glancing up at the sky. 'Looks as though there won't be any difficulty about that.'

Out of breath, Merle turned, too slowly because her dress hampered her movements in the water. Then she saw what he meant.

'Dive!' she shouted, and didn't see whether Serafin was doing as she said. She herself held her breath and slid under the water, tasting it, cold and salty, on her lips, feeling the pressure in her ears and nose. The canal must be about three metres deep, and she knew she had to get at least half that depth between herself and the lions' claws.

She could see and hear nothing of what was going on around her, but she turned to a horizontal position and swam a few vigorous strokes along the canal. Perhaps she could make it if she reached one of the old loading doors.

Back in the old days, when Venice was still a great trading city, the merchants used to have their wares brought from the canals into their houses through doors set level with the surface of the water. Many of those houses might be empty today, their owners dead and gone, but the doors still stood there, most of them rotten, eroded by salt water. Often the whole bottom part of a door had rotted away. One of them would make an ideal bolthole for Merle.

What about Serafin?

She could only pray that he was following and was not too far above her, where the lions' paws could seize him even in the water. Stone lions do not like water and never did, and the last flying specimens of their kind were no exception. They might dip their claws into the canal, but they would never, never dive right in. Merle knew about this weakness of the lions, and she hoped with all her might that Serafin did too.

She was beginning to run out of air, and in her need she put up a quick prayer to the Flowing Queen. Then she remembered that the Queen was in a flask in the pocket of her dress, held captive there like a genie in a fairy tale, and probably as helpless as Merle herself.

The essence of the Flowing Queen, that was what the councillor had said.

Where was Serafin? And where could she find a door?

Her senses were failing. The blackness around her seemed to be moving in circles, and she felt as if she were falling down and down, although in fact she was drifting up towards the surface.

She broke through it. Air streamed into her lungs. She opened her eyes.

She had come further than she'd hoped. There really was a door quite near, rough-edged and splintered where the water had lapped and lapped at the wood, finally eating it away. The upper half of the door hung intact on its hinges, but beneath it gaped a black hole giving access to the inside of the house. The rotten wood looked like the jaws of a sea monster, a row of sharp spikes, crumbling away and green with seaweed and mould.

'*Merle!*'

Serafin's voice made her spin round in the water. What she saw numbed her from head to foot. She almost sank.

One of the lions, hovering above the water, was holding the dripping figure of Serafin in its forepaws, like a fish it had caught and plucked from the waves.

'Merle!' shouted Serafin again. She realised that he couldn't see her, didn't know where she was or even if she was still alive. He was afraid for her. Afraid she had drowned.

Everything in her clamoured to answer, to draw the lions' attention away from him and perhaps give him a chance to escape. But she knew she was only deceiving herself. Once a lion has caught its prey, it does not let go.

The creature was already turning with purposeful wing-beats, flying away, climbing higher, holding the defenceless Serafin firmly under its body.

'Merle, wherever you are, you must get away!' cried Serafin in a voice that was growing fainter and fainter. 'Hide! Save the Flowing Queen!'

And with that the lion, his rider and Serafin vanished into the night like a cloud of ash dispersed by the wind.

Merle dived down. Her tears mingled with the water of the canal, became one with it like Merle herself. She plunged into that mouth full of wooden teeth, passing through the rotten door into even deeper blackness, until she found herself in the dark but in the dry. She curled up like a small child, and just lay there, weeping.

Breathing and weeping.

AN END AND A BEGINNING

The Flowing Queen spoke to her.

'*Merle*,' said her voice. '*Merle, listen to me!*'

Merle came to herself with a start, her gaze searching the darkness. The old warehouse smelled of moisture and rotten wood. The only light came in from the canal through the dilapidated door. There was a glimmering and flickering in the air – someone outside was searching the surface of the water with torches.

She must get away from here as quickly as possible.

'*You're not dreaming, Merle*.'

The words were inside her; the voice was speaking in her head.

'Who are you?' she whispered, leaping to her feet.

'*You know who I am. Don't be afraid of me*.'

Merle's hand took the mirror out of the pocket of her dress and held it up in the flickering torchlight. The surface was smooth, the phantom was nowhere to be seen. But she guessed it wasn't the phantom speaking to her anyway. She quickly slid the mirror back into her pocket and took out the flask. It fitted comfortably in her hand.

'You?' If she said only single words and not whole sentences, perhaps the way her voice was shaking wouldn't be too obvious.

'You must get away from here. They'll be searching all the buildings on the bank of the canal. And after that they'll search the rest of the quarter.'

'What about Serafin?'

'He is a prisoner of the Guard now.'

'They'll kill him!'

'Perhaps. But not at once. They could have done that in the water. They'll try to find out who you are and where they can track you down.'

Merle put the flask back in her pocket and groped her way through the dark. She was freezing cold in her wet dress, but her goosebumps had nothing to do with the temperature.

'Are you the Flowing Queen?' she asked softly.

'Is that what you want to call me? A queen?'

'What I want to do most is get away from here.'

'Then that's what we ought to do.'

'We? I can see only one person here with legs to run away on.'

In the dark, she found a door leading further down into the building. She slipped through it and straight into an abandoned entrance hall. The floor and the banisters of the stairs were covered with a thick layer of dust. Merle's feet left tracks in the dirt as they would in snow. It wouldn't be difficult for her pursuers to get on her trail.

The front door of the house was nailed up from the outside, like so many doors in Venice these days, but she found a window with a pane that she could break, using the fallen head of a statue. By some miracle she didn't cut her hands or knees climbing out.

Now what? She'd better get back to the Outcasts' Canal. Arcimboldo would know what to do. Or Eft. Or Junipa. Someone would, anyway! She couldn't carry this secret about with her all by herself.

'*If your friend talks, that's where they'll look for you first*,' the voice abruptly warned her.

'Serafin won't give me away,' she replied angrily. And in her thoughts she added: He swore never to let me down.

She, on the other hand, had stood by and watched as the lion carried him away. But what could she have done?

'*Nothing*,' said the voice. '*You were helpless. You still are.*'

'Are you reading my mind?'

She got no answer to that, which was answer enough in itself.

'Well, don't,' she said sharply. 'I rescued you. You owe me something.'

More silence. Had she annoyed the voice? Good; then it might leave her in peace. It was hard enough thinking for just one person. She didn't need a second, inner voice finding fault with all her decisions.

Cautiously she went down an alley, stopping again and again, listening for pursuers and suspicious sounds. She kept an eye on the sky too, although it was so dark that a whole pride of lions could have been flying overhead for all she knew. It was still hours before sunrise.

Soon she knew where she was: just a few streets away from the Campo San Paolo. She had covered half the distance back to the workshop. Not much further and she'd be in safety.

'*There isn't any safety*,' the voice contradicted her. '*Not while the boy is still a prisoner.*'

Merle lost her temper. 'What is all this?' she cried, and her voice echoed back from the walls. 'What are you? The voice of reason?'

'That too, if you like.'

'I'd just like you to leave me alone!'

'I'm giving you advice, not orders.'

'I don't need advice.'

'I'm very much afraid you do.'

Merle stopped, looked round furiously, and found a wooden hoarding between two buildings. There was a gap in it. She had to clear this up once and for all. Here and now. She wriggled through the gap, went a little further into the dark space between the walls of the buildings, and then sat down with her knees drawn up.

'You want to talk to me? Right, then let's talk.'

'As you please.'

'Who or what are you?'

'I think you know that already.'

'The Flowing Queen?'

'At the moment I'm only a voice inside your head.'

Merle hesitated. If the voice really did belong to the Flowing Queen, might it be a good idea to show her a little more respect? But she still had her doubts. 'You don't talk like a queen.'

'I talk as you do. I'm speaking with your voice and your thoughts.'

'I'm just an ordinary girl.'

'You're more than that now. You have undertaken a task.'

'I haven't undertaken anything!' said Merle. 'I never asked for any of this. And don't go telling me about destiny and all that guff. This isn't a fairy tale.'

'I'm afraid not. Everything's simpler in a fairy tale. You go home, you find that the soldiers have burned down your house and taken your friends away, you're angry, you realise that you must take up the struggle against the Pharaoh, finally you meet him and through a cunning ruse you kill him. That's how the fairy tale would run. But unfortunately we're dealing with real life. The way you must go is the same, yet different.'

'I could simply take the flask and tip its contents into the nearest canal.'

'No! That would kill me!'

'So you're not the Flowing Queen, then! She's perfectly at home in the canals.'

'The Flowing Queen is only what you wish her to be. At the moment, a little liquid in a flask and a voice inside your head.'

'That doesn't make sense. I don't understand you.'

'The Egyptians drove me out of the canals by casting a spell on the water. But for that, the traitors could never have imprisoned me in this flask. The magic is still in the water of the lagoon, and it

will take months to disperse. Until then my essence must not join the water.'

'We all thought you were something . . . something else.'

'Sorry to disappoint you.'

'Something – well, spiritual.'

'Like God?'

'Yes, I suppose so.'

'Even God is only inside people who believe in him. The way I'm inside you now.'

'That's not the same thing. You're leaving me no choice. You're talking to me. I *have* to believe in you, or . . .'

'Or what?'

'Or it means I've gone crazy. It means I'm just talking to myself.'

'Would that be so bad? Listening to the voice inside you?'

Merle shook her head impatiently. 'That's splitting hairs. You're just trying to confuse me. Perhaps you're really only the stupid phantom that flew into my mirror.'

'Put me to the test. Leave the mirror somewhere, part with it. Then you'll find out that I'm still with you.'

'I'd never part with my mirror of my own free will, and I think you know that perfectly well.'

'I don't mean for ever, just for a moment. Put it down at the far

end of this passageway between the buildings, come back, and listen to find out if I'm still here.'

Merle considered briefly and then agreed. She took the mirror to the far end of the narrow space, about fifteen metres from the way in. She had to clamber over all kinds of rubbish that had accumulated here over the years, and kicked out at the rats snapping at her heels. Finally she went back to the gap in the hoarding without her mirror.

'Well?' she asked quietly.

'*Here I am*,' said the voice, sounding amused.

Merle sighed. 'Does that mean you still claim to be the Flowing Queen?'

'*I never said so. You did.*'

Merle hurried back to her mirror, picked it up, quickly put it in the pocket of her dress and did up the button on the pocket. 'You said you were using my words and my thoughts. Does that mean you can influence my will too?'

'*I wouldn't even if I could.*'

'So I suppose I have to believe you, right?'

'*Trust me.*'

It was the second time tonight someone had asked her to do that. She didn't like it at all.

'All the same, I could be simply imagining things, couldn't I?'

'Which would you rather? An imaginary voice speaking to you or a real one?'

'Neither.'

'I won't call on your services any longer than necessary.'

Merle opened her eyes wide. 'My *services?*'

'I need your help. The Egyptian spy and the traitors will stop at nothing to get me back in their power. They'll hunt you down. We must leave Venice.'

'Leave the city? But that's impossible! The besiegers have been surrounding it for over thirty years, and it's said that the ring encircling us is still as impenetrable as it was on the first day.'

The voice sounded sad. *'I did my best, but in the end I myself fell victim to the cunning of the enemy. I can't protect the lagoon any longer. We must find another way.'*

'But – but what about all the people? And the mermaids?'

'No one can stop the Egyptians invading now. At the moment, they're still not sure what's become of me. That will help us to get a start on them. But it won't be long before they find out the truth, and after that the city is no longer safe.'

'So we just have a reprieve.'

'*Yes*,' said the voice sadly. '*No more and no less. But if the Pharaoh closes in on the lagoon, he'll be looking for you. The envoy knows your face. He won't rest until you're dead.*'

Merle thought of Junipa and Serafin, Arcimboldo and Eft. Of all the people who meant something to her. Was she to leave them behind and run away?

'*Not run away*,' the voice contradicted her. '*Set out on our quest. I am the lagoon. I will never give it up. If it dies, I die too. But we must leave the city and find help.*'

'There's no one left out there to help us. The Empire has ruled the whole world for ages.'

'*Perhaps. Or perhaps not.*'

Merle had had enough of these mysterious hints, although by now she hardly doubted that the voice in her head really did belong to the Flowing Queen. And in spite of growing up in a city where the Queen was venerated so much, she found she couldn't feel in awe of her. She, Merle, had never asked to be dragged into all this.

'I'm going back to the workshop first,' she said. 'I have to speak to Junipa and Arcimboldo.'

'*We'll lose valuable time.*'

'That's what I've decided!' snapped Merle angrily.

'Just as you like.'

'You mean you're not going to try to make me change my mind?'

'*No.*'

That surprised her, but it did restore a little of her self-confidence. She was about to scramble through the gap in the hoarding and back into the alleyway when the voice spoke up again.

'There's something else.'

'Yes?'

'I can't stay in this flask much longer.'

'Why not?'

'The desert crystal is paralysing my thoughts.'

Merle smiled. 'Does that mean you won't talk so much?'

'It means I shall die. My essence must be linked to living organisms. The water of the lagoon is full of them. But the flask is made of cold, dead crystal. I shall wither like a plant deprived of soil and light.'

'How can I help you?'

'You must drink me.'

Merle made a face. 'Er . . . drink you?'

'We must become one, you and I.'

'You're in my head already, so now you want my whole

body too? Ever heard that proverb about giving someone an inch and they take . . .'

'I shall die, Merle. And the lagoon will die with me.'

'That's blackmail, do you realise? If I don't help you, everyone will die. If I don't drink you, everyone will die. What's the next bit?'

'Drink me, Merle.'

She took the flask out of her pocket. The cut-crystal facets sparkled like an insect's eye. 'Is there no other way?'

'No, none.'

'How will you . . . I mean, how are you going to get out of me again? And when?'

'When the time comes.'

'I kind of thought you'd say something like that.'

'I wouldn't ask you if we had any choice.'

For a brief moment it occurred to Merle that she herself did have a choice. She could still throw the flask away and act as if tonight's events had never happened. But how could she pretend to herself that they hadn't? Serafin, the fight with the Egyptian envoy, the Flowing Queen, all of it.

Sometimes responsibility creeps up on you when you never saw it coming, and then, all of a sudden, it won't let go again.

Merle took the stopper out of the flask and sniffed it. Nothing, no smell at all.

'What . . . er, what do you taste like?'

'*Anything you fancy.*'

'How about fresh raspberries?'

'*Why not?*'

After one final moment of hesitation, Merle raised the open flask to her mouth and drank. The liquid inside was as clear and cool as water. Two or three mouthfuls, no more, and then the flask was empty.

'It didn't taste of raspberries!'

'*What did it taste of?*'

'Nothing at all.'

'*Then it wasn't as bad as you expected, was it?*'

'I hate it when people tell me lies.'

'*It won't happen again. Do you feel any different now?*'

Merle tried listening to her inner self, but she could detect no change. It might just as well have been plain water in the flask.

'No, I feel the same as before.'

'*Good. Then throw the empty flask away now. It mustn't be found on you.*'

Merle put the stopper back in the little crystal container

and pushed it under a heap of rubbish. She was gradually taking in what had just happened.

'Do I really have the Flowing Queen inside me now?'

'*You always had her inside you. Like everyone who believes in her.*'

'That sounds like church and priests and religious stuff.'

The voice in her head sighed. '*If it makes you feel better, yes, I am inside you. Really inside you.*'

Merle frowned, and then shrugged her shoulders. 'I suppose there's nothing to be done about it now.'

The voice did not reply. Merle took her chance to leave her hiding place at last. She ran along the streets to the Outcasts' Canal as fast as she could go, keeping close to the walls of the buildings so as not to be seen from the air. The sky was probably swarming with the lions of the Guard by now.

'*I shouldn't think so,*' the Flowing Queen disagreed. '*Only three of the city councillors betrayed me, and they have to be content with their own share of the bodyguard. No councillor has more than two flying lions at his disposal, which makes six lions in all at the very most.*'

'Six lions doing nothing but look for me?' exclaimed Merle. 'Is that supposed to make me feel better? Thanks very much!'

'You're welcome.'

'You don't know much about us human beings, do you?'

'I've never had a chance to find out more about you.'

Merle silently shook her head. The Flowing Queen had been venerated in the city for decades, there were cults devoted to her worship alone. And the Queen herself knew nothing about it. Nothing about human beings or all she meant to them.

She was the lagoon. But did that make her a goddess too?

'Is the Pharaoh a god because the Egyptians worship him like one?' asked the voice. *'He may be a god to them. He isn't to you Venetians. Divinity is in the eye of the beholder.'*

Merle was not in any mood to stop and think about divinity, so she asked, 'That business with the mirror just now – that was you, wasn't it?'

'No.'

'Then was it the mirror itself? Or the phantom in the mirror?'

'Have you thought that you might have thrown it at the envoy yourself?'

'I'd know about it if I had.'

'You hear a voice in your head that may be only yours. Perhaps you do things without being aware of it too – simply because they're right.'

'Nonsense.'

'*As you like.*'

They said no more about it, but Merle couldn't shake off the idea. Suppose she really was just imagining the voice of the Flowing Queen? Talking to an illusion all this time? And even worse, suppose she no longer had control over her own actions and was crediting them with supernatural powers that didn't actually exist?

The thought frightened her more than the way a strange being had taken up residence inside her. On the other hand, she didn't feel the presence of the strange being at all. It was dreadfully confusing.

Merle reached the mouth of the Outcasts' Canal. The party wasn't over yet; a few tireless merrymakers were sitting on the bridge, talking quietly or staring silently into their mugs. Junipa and the boys were nowhere to be seen. They had probably gone home hours ago.

Merle walked down the narrow path along the canal bank until she reached Arcimboldo's workshop. The water whispered as it lapped against the stone. She looked up at the night sky one last time, imagining the lions circling in the air above the light of all the gas lamps and torches. The soldiers riding them might not be able to see in the dark, but cats were nocturnal animals, weren't they? In her mind she saw the yellow eyes of the beasts of prey staring down, full of bloodlust, in search of a girl in wet, torn clothes, with straggling hair and knowledge that could mean her death.

She knocked at the door. No one answered. She knocked again. The sounds seemed louder than usual; they must be audible throughout this whole quarter. Perhaps a lion was already on the way, nosediving through the cold air, then through the haze above the city, through the smoke of fires and chimneys, the faint light of lanterns, and making straight for Merle. She looked up at the dark above her in alarm. Perhaps there really was something there, gigantic stone wings, paws as big as puppies and –

The door opened. Eft seized her arm and pulled her into the house.

'What did you think you were doing, running off like that?' The mermaid's eyes flashed angrily as she slammed the door behind Merle. 'I expected you, of all people, to have more sense than to –'

'I must speak to the Master.' Merle looked back anxiously at the door.

'There was no one there,' the Queen reassured her.

'Speak to the Master?' asked Eft. She obviously couldn't hear the voice. 'Have you any idea how late it is?'

'I'm sorry. I really am. But it's important.'

She held Eft's gaze and tried to read the mermaid's eyes. You have been touched by the Flowing Queen, Eft had told her. In retrospect, it sounded almost like a prophecy, one that had come true tonight. Could Eft feel the change that had come over Merle? Did she sense the presence of a stranger in her mind?

Whatever the reason, Eft stopped scolding Merle. Instead, she turned and said, 'Come with me.'

They went to the workshop door in silence. Eft left Merle there. 'Arcimboldo is still at work. He works every night. Tell him whatever it is you have to say.' With that she disappeared into the darkness, and soon the sound of her footsteps died away.

Merle was left alone outside the door. It cost her an effort to raise her hand and knock. What could she tell Arcimboldo? The whole truth? Wouldn't he think she was mad and throw her out of the house? Even worse: wouldn't he instantly realise what a threat she represented to the workshop and the people living there?

All the same, she felt a curious certainty that it was right to talk to him rather than Eft. The mermaid revered the Flowing Queen. Merle's story would sound to her like blasphemy, the idle talk of a girl trying to make herself seem important.

Footsteps sounded on the other side of the door. It opened and Arcimboldo looked out. 'Merle! You're back!'

She hadn't expected him even to have noticed her absence. Eft must have told him.

'Come in, come in!' Hastily, he beckoned her into the workshop. 'We've been so worried about you.'

Well, that was something new. In the orphanage, Merle had never known them to worry about anyone. If one of the children disappeared, a half-hearted and usually unsuccessful search was made, but it meant one mouth less to feed, one more vacancy.

It was warm in the workshop. Little white clouds of steam puffed out of Arcimboldo's apparatus, which was all linked together by a tangle of pipes, tubes and glass globes. The mirror-maker used these machines only by night, when he was alone. By day he worked in the traditional manner, perhaps because he didn't want his pupils to see too far into the secrets of his art. Did he ever sleep? Hard to say. In Merle's eyes, Arcimboldo was one of the fixtures of the workshop, like the oak door and the tall windows with their dusty panes on which generations of apprentices had scratched their initials.

Arcimboldo went over to one of his pieces of apparatus, adjusted a regulator and then turned back to her. Behind him, the machine emitted three clouds of steam in short bursts. 'Now, tell me. Where have you been?'

On the way back, Merle had thought a good deal about what she was going tell Arcimboldo. It had not been an easy decision to make. 'I don't think you'll understand me.'

'Never mind that. I just want to hear the truth.'

She took a deep breath. 'I've come back to say thank you. And so that you'll know I'm all right.'

'It sounds as if you're planning to leave us.'

'I'm leaving Venice.'

She had expected all kinds of reactions to her news: she'd thought he might laugh at her, be angry, or lock her up. She hadn't expected the grief that now darkened his gaze. No anger, no harsh words, just plain sorrow. 'What has happened?'

She told him everything, beginning with her meeting with Serafin, going on to the scuffle in the empty building, and so to the story of the flask containing the Flowing

Queen and Serafin's capture. She described the robes and faces of the three traitors, and he nodded sadly at each description, as if he knew exactly who they were. She told him about the voice in her head and, sounding slightly ashamed, she told him how she had drunk the contents of the flask.

When she had finished, Arcimboldo sat down on a wooden stool, still looking distressed. He mopped sweat from his brow with a cloth, blew his nose on it vigorously, and then threw it into the opening of the stove. They both watched as the flames consumed the fabric, and they preserved an almost devout silence as if something else were burning there: a memory, perhaps, or the thought of what might have been – but for the Egyptians, but for the traitors and the magic poison that had driven the Flowing Queen from the canals.

'You are right,' said Arcimboldo after a while. 'It's not safe for you here. It's not safe anywhere in Venice. But in you the Flowing Queen can leave the lagoon, for you were born here and so you are a part of her.'

'You know more about her than you've ever told us,' she remarked.

He smiled sadly. 'A little. She was always an important

part of my work. Without her there will be no more magic mirrors.'

'But that means that . . .'

'That sooner or later I must close the workshop, yes. The water of the lagoon is one component of my art. Without the breath of the Flowing Queen, which goes into every mirror, all my skill is useless.'

An uneasy feeling clutched at Merle's heart. 'What about the others? Junipa and Boro and . . .' There was a lump in her throat. 'Will they have to go back to a Home?'

Arcimboldo thought for a moment, then shook his head. 'No, not that. But who knows what will happen when the Egyptians march in? No one can say in advance. Perhaps there will be fighting, and then I'm sure the boys will want to join in on the defending side.' He rubbed both hands over his face. 'As if that would do any good.'

Merle wished the Flowing Queen would come up with some kind of answer. A few comforting words, something, anything! But the voice inside her was silent, and she had no idea how she herself could cheer the mirror-maker.

'You must go on looking after Junipa,' she said. 'Promise me.'

'Of course.' But to Merle's ears, his assurance didn't

sound anything like as convincing as she could have wished.

'Do you think the Egyptians are a threat to her? Because of her eyes?'

'In all the countries invaded by the Empire, the sick, injured and weak have always been the first to suffer. The Pharaoh puts healthy men and women to work in his factories, but as for the rest . . . I can't answer your question, Merle.'

'But Junipa *must* be all right!' Merle couldn't understand how she had ever thought of leaving without saying goodbye to Junipa. She must go to her as quickly as possible. Perhaps she could even take Junipa with her . . .

'*No,*' the Flowing Queen interrupted. '*You can't do that.*'

'Why not?' asked Merle defiantly. Arcimboldo looked up, thinking she had spoken to him. But then he saw that her gaze was turned inwards, and he knew who she was talking to.

'*The way we must go is hard enough for one person alone. The old man has promised to look after your friend.*'

'But I –'

'*It can't be done.*'

'Don't keep interrupting me!'

'*You must believe me. She's in safety here. Out there you'd only be putting her in danger unnecessarily. In fact you'd both be in danger.'*

'Both of us?' asked Merle sharply. 'You mean, I'd be putting *you* in danger!'

'Merle!' Arcimboldo had risen to his feet. He took her by the shoulders. 'If you're really talking to the Flowing Queen, that's not the proper tone to adopt!'

'Huh!' She took a step back. Suddenly there were tears in her eyes. 'What do you know about it? Junipa's my friend! I can't just leave her in the lurch!'

She stepped back again, rubbing her eyes angrily. She wasn't going to cry. Not here, not now.

'You're not leaving me in the lurch!' said a voice behind her, a very soft and quiet voice.

Merle spun round. 'Junipa!'

In the darkness of the open workshop doorway, the silver eyes sparkled like a pair of stars fallen from the sky. Junipa stepped in. The yellow flickering of the fire in the stove cast a wavering light on her thin features. She was wearing her white nightdress, with a red shawl thrown over it.

'I couldn't sleep,' she said. 'I was so worried about you. Eft came to tell me I'd find you here.'

Dear, kind Eft, thought Merle gratefully. She'd never show it openly, but she knows exactly what's going on in all our minds.

Relieved, she gave Junipa a hug. It was good to see her friend and hear her voice. She felt as if they hadn't seen each other for weeks, although she had left Junipa at the party only a few hours before.

When Merle let go of her friend again, she looked straight into Junipa's mirror-glass eyes. The sight no longer troubled her; she had seen much worse things now.

'I was listening at the door,' Junipa confessed with the ghost of a smile. 'Eft showed me how.' She pointed back over her shoulder, and there stood Eft in the dark corridor. She raised an eyebrow but said nothing.

Merle couldn't help it: she laughed, little though she felt like laughing. She no longer had control of herself, she just laughed and laughed . . .

'Did you hear everything?' she finally gasped. 'Both of you?'

Junipa nodded, while Eft suppressed a smile, but otherwise stood stock still.

'Then you must think I'm crazy.'

'No,' said Junipa gravely, and Eft whispered, under

her breath, 'The one touched by the Flowing Queen has come home to say goodbye. The way of the hero is just beginning.'

Merle did not feel at all like a hero, and she didn't even want to think about the fact that all this might be merely the start of something more. But secretly, of course, she knew that Eft was right. A farewell, a beginning, and then a journey. Her journey.

Junipa took her hand and held it tight. 'I will stay here with Arcimboldo and Eft. You go where you must go.'

'Junipa, do you still remember what you told me on our first night here?'

'That I'd never been anything but a nuisance to everyone?'

Merle nodded. 'But you aren't! And you wouldn't be if you came with me!'

Junipa's smile was brighter than the cool silver of her eyes. 'I know. A great many things have changed since that night. Arcimboldo will need my help, particularly if it really comes to fighting between the Venetians and the Egyptians. The boys will be the first to join any resistance movement.'

'You must stop them.'

'You know Dario,' sighed Arcimboldo. 'He won't let anyone keep him out of a good brawl.'

'But war is not a brawl!'

'He won't understand that. And Boro and Tiziano will join him.' The mirror-maker looked very old and grey now, as if it cost him dear to admit his powerlessness. 'Junipa will give us valuable aid. In every way.'

Merle wondered whether Arcimboldo loved Eft as a man loves a woman. Did he think of Junipa as the daughter he and the mermaid would never have?

And who was she to try guessing at other people's feelings? She had never had a family, didn't know what it was like to have a mother and father of her own. But perhaps Junipa would if she, Merle, gave Arcimboldo and Eft the chance.

It was right to go alone. Just Merle and the Flowing Queen. Junipa's place was here, in this house with these people.

She hugged her friend again, and then put her arms around Arcimboldo and finally around Eft too. 'Goodbye!' she said. 'We'll all meet again some time.'

'Do you know the way?' asked Junipa.

'I'll show her,' said Eft, before Merle could reply.

Arcimboldo nodded his agreement.

Merle and the mermaid exchanged a glance. Eft's eyes were bright, but perhaps that was only because of the sharp contrast they made with the shadow cast on her features by the rim of her mask.

Junipa took Merle's hands one last time. 'Good luck,' she said huskily. 'Look after yourself.'

'The Flowing Queen is with me.' The words came out before Merle could even form the intention of speaking them. She wondered if the Queen had helped her, as a comfort for Junipa.

'Come on now,' said Eft, and walked quickly down the corridor.

After a few metres Merle looked behind her once more, back at the workshop door. There stood Junipa beside Arcimboldo. For a strange moment Merle saw herself standing beside the mirror-maker, with his arm around her shoulders. But then her likeness changed back into the girl with the mirror-glass eyes, the figure's dark hair turned blond, she became thinner again and more vulnerable.

Eft led Merle into the inner courtyard, straight to the cistern, down into the depths.

The shaft of the well received her. It felt like a living thing and, despite the cool stone around her, Merle grew warm.

Yes, she thought, this is how it could begin. This is how it really could begin.

ALONG THE CANALS

Mermaids! So many mermaids!

In the grey-green twilight their fish-tails shone with a silvery gleam, like the flickering of glow-worms on a summer night. Two of them held Merle's hands and drew her along the canals with them.

Eft had climbed down into the cistern with Merle. It had taken the girl a little while to realise that the slight turbulence round her legs was not just the water itself. Something was moving, swirling fast around her, feeling her with the lightest of fingers, with a touch more delicate than a dog's nose sniffing at a stranger, very carefully, very gently. She felt as if the fingers were touching her far below her skin, as if someone were reading her mind.

Eft said a few words in the curious language of the merfolk. They echoed back, strange and mysterious, from the walls of the well shaft, and went deep down under the surface to the ears of those who understood them and knew what they had to do.

A pale hand came up out of the water in front of Merle and gave her a globe of veined glass. It seemed to be a kind of helmet. Eft helped her to put it over her head and tie its little leather strap tightly under her chin. Merle was not afraid now, not in this place and with these beings.

'*I am with you*,' said the Flowing Queen. To her, this was a homecoming to her own realm, caught as she was in Merle's body, yet protected by it from the poison of the Egyptian magicians.

Eft had stayed behind in the well, and now Merle was swimming along the canals with the shoal of mermaids. Where were they taking her? How was it that she could breathe inside the glass globe? And why did a pleasant warmth radiate from the mermaids, keeping Merle from freezing in the icy water?

Questions upon questions, and more kept coming, an army of doubts forming in her mind.

'*I can tell you the answers to some of them*,' said the Flowing Queen.

Merle dared not speak for fear of using up the air inside the glass helmet.

'*You don't need to speak aloud for me to hear you*,' said the

Queen within Merle. *'I thought you'd realised that by now.'*

Merle tried to form clear sentences inside her head. 'How long can I breathe with this thing on?'

'As long as you like.'

'Does Eft use it too when she climbs down into the well by night?'

'Yes, but it wasn't made for her. It comes from a time when the merfolk still had their old knowledge, from the old days when water was everywhere and the oceans teemed with an infinite diversity of life. Much remains from those days, buried in the old cities beneath the waves, in the deep trenches and fissures of the seabed. At that time, countless years ago, expeditions were sometimes sent out to those sunken cities, and now and then they brought back treasures like this helmet.'

'Is it technology or magic?'

'What is magic but a kind of technology that most people don't understand? Either they don't understand it yet or they don't understand it any more.' For a moment, the Queen seemed to be amused by her own words and then she was grave again. *'But you're not entirely wrong. From your point of view it's more magic than technology. What looks to you like glass is really solidified water.'*

'Arcimboldo said something about using the water of the

lagoon to make his magic mirrors. And he said he can only work with it if your breath is in it.'

'*He uses a similar process. Outwardly, his mirrors look as if they are made of ordinary glass. In truth, however, their surface is an alloy of solidified water. Thousands of years ago, in the age of the sub-oceanic realms, craftsmen worked with water as you humans work with wood and metal today. Other days, other kinds of knowledge! Arcimboldo is one of the few who can still work with it today – although even his skill is a mere shadow of what the old sub-oceanic craftsmen could do. And Arcimboldo told the truth: my presence made the water of the lagoon what it was. Without me it cannot solidify.*'

Merle nodded thoughtfully. All the Flowing Queen's explanations were leading to the same conclusion. 'Are you one of these sub-oceanic people yourself – one of the old people who lived under the sea?'

The Queen was silent for quite a long time, while the mermaids' shimmering fish-tails danced around Merle in the dark.

'*I am old,*' she said at last. '*Infinitely older than all the life in the sea.*'

There was something in the Flowing Queen's tone that made Merle doubt her. What she said was certainly no lie –

but was it the whole truth? Merle knew that at this moment the Queen was reading her thoughts, so she knew about her doubts too. But for some reason or other, the Queen did not pursue the point further. Instead, she changed the subject.

'Just now you wanted to know where the mermaids were taking us.'

'Out of the lagoon?'

'No, they can't do that. The danger would be too great. If an Egyptian reconnaissance craft saw a whole shoal of them under the surface, it would go after them. We can't risk that. Too many of the merfolk have already died at human hands – I won't ask them to give their lives for their oppressors now.'

Fascinated, Merle couldn't take her eyes off the slender bodies flocking around her, guiding her safely along the deep canals. Comforting warmth radiated from the hands of the two mermaids drawing her gently through the water.

'They're taking us to the Piazza San Marco,' said the Queen.

'But that's –'

'In the very centre of the city. Yes, I know.'

'And we'll run straight into the arms of the guard there!'

'Not if I can help it.'

'Look, it's *my* body, don't forget that! I'm the one who'll have to run away. And be tortured. And killed.'

'We have no alternative. There's only one way for us to leave the city, and there's someone there who can help us.'

'In the Piazza San Marco, of all places?'

'I tell you, we don't have any choice, Merle. It's the only place where we can meet him. He's . . . well, he's held prisoner there.'

Merle nearly choked. Next to the Piazza San Marco lay the old Doge's Palace, once the residence of the rulers of Venice and now the headquarters of the City Council. The palace dungeons were legendary, both the prison cells beneath its lead roofs and the large prison on the other side of the canal, which could be reached from the Palace only over the Bridge of Sighs. Those who crossed that bridge never saw the light of day again.

'Are you seriously planning to free a prisoner from the dungeons of the Doge's Palace to help us leave Venice? We might just as well jump straight off the nearest tower!'

'You're closer to the truth than you know, Merle. The prisoner who will help us is held captive not in the dungeons but in the Campanile.'

'The tallest tower in the city!'

'Yes, it is.'

The Campanile stood in the Piazza San Marco and towered above all Venice. Merle was still at a loss to think what the Queen was planning. 'But there isn't any prison in the Campanile!'

'Not for common criminals. Do you remember the legends?'

'What's your friend's name?'

'Vermithrax. But you are more likely to know him as –'

'The Traitor of Old!'

'That's right.'

'But it's only a story. An old wives' tale. Vermithrax never really existed.'

'I doubt if he'd agree with you.'

Merle closed her eyes for a few seconds. She had to concentrate, she mustn't make any mistakes now. Her life depended on it.

Vermithrax, the Traitor of Old! He was a figure of myth and legend, his name was spoken as a curse. But a living, breathing being – no, impossible! Magic and sea-witches were real enough, part of Merle's everyday environment. Vermithrax, though? It was as if someone had told her she'd just had lunch with God in person.

Or had drunk the essence of the Flowing Queen.

'Very well,' sighed Merle in her thoughts, 'so you're saying the Traitor of Old is held prisoner in the Campanile in the Piazza San Marco, is that right?'

'You have my word for it.'

'And the idea is, we simply go there, set him free – and then what?'

'You'll find out when we're with him. He owes me a favour.'

'Vermithrax owes you something?'

'I helped him once, many years ago.'

'Well, that obviously got him a long way – straight to prison!'

'Your sarcasm is misplaced, my dear.'

Resigned, Merle shook her head. One of the mermaids glanced at her to make sure that all was well. Merle gave her a small smile. The mermaid returned it with her wide, shark-like muzzle, and turned her eyes forward again.

'If he's been held prisoner there all these years, how come no one knows about it?'

'Oh, everyone knows.'

'But they think it's just a legend!'

'Because that's what they want to think. Perhaps far more fairy tales and myths would turn out to be true if only someone could summon up the courage to search for a golden ball at the bottom of a well, or cut a way through the thorny hedge outside a castle.'

Merle thought about it. 'He really is up there?'

'He is.'

'He must be closely guarded. So how are you going to set him free?'

'*With a little luck*,' replied the Queen.

Merle was about to answer back when she felt the mermaids rising towards the surface. Above her she could see the keels of gondolas, ranged side by side, rocking gently on the waves. Merle knew where they were: at the gondola moorings of the Piazza San Marco.

The water around the gondolas was tinged with a red-gold glow. The dawn sky, thought Merle, relieved. Sunrise. Her mood lifted a little, although daylight would make it more difficult for them to reach the Campanile.

'*Too early*,' the Flowing Queen disagreed. She sounded anxious. '*Too early for sunrise.*'

'But the light!'

'*It's shining from the west. The sun rises in the east.*'

'What is it, then?'

The Flowing Queen was silent for a moment, while the mermaids, at a loss, waited a few metres below the surface of the water.

'*Fire*,' she said at last. '*The Piazza San Marco is on fire!*'

THE FIERY ENVOY

Three metres above the ground, the lion opened its claws and let him drop. Serafin arched his back in the air and landed safely on hands and feet, thanks to the thousands of similar drops he had made from high windows, rooftop balustrades and terraces. Perhaps he wasn't a Master Thief of the Guild any more, but he hadn't forgotten his old skills.

Quick as a flash he rose, leaning slightly forward, ready to fight, when two guards aimed their rifles at him and put paid to any idea of resistance. Serafin let his breath out abruptly, then stretched and relaxed his muscles. He was a prisoner: it might be wiser not to be too stroppy. He'd need all his strength later, when they carted him off to the jailer and the torturers. No point wearing himself out on a couple of guardsmen.

With a gesture of resignation, he held out both his wrists to be handcuffed. But that wasn't what the men had in mind. They just went on pointing their guns at him. Only a boy. Not worth the trouble of handcuffs.

Serafin suppressed a smile. He wasn't scared. As long as he was in the open air, not in a dungeon and well away from the Bridge of Sighs, the last road ever trodden by condemned men, he was not afraid. His self-confidence was a shield that he held raised aloft to keep him from thinking about Merle – although he did not entirely succeed there.

Surely nothing bad had happened to her! She was alive and safe! Those thoughts became a creed that he kept reciting deep in his heart.

Concentrate on what's around you, he told himself. And ask yourself a few questions, like why did we land here and not in the prison courtyard?

It was, in fact, surprising. The lion had dropped him on the edge of the Piazza San Marco, where the two guardsmen were ready and waiting for him. They were now joined by two more. All four men wore the black leather uniform of the City Guard, studded with rivets that reflected the light of several braziers on the bank of the canal nearby.

The Piazza San Marco was an extended L-shaped area in the centre of Venice. One end of the piazza adjoined the water. Nearby was the Canal Grande, and on the opposite side of the canal the roofs and towers of the Giudecca island rose into the night sky.

The piazza was surrounded by magnificent buildings, the most impressive being the Basilica of St Mark, a mighty structure of domes and turrets. The gold and the statues that adorned it had been brought back from all over the world by Venetian seamen centuries ago. Some described it as a house of God, some called it the pirates' cathedral.

Next to the Basilica of St Mark was the facade of the Doge's Palace, where no prince had ruled for many years now. Today the councillors decided on the city's policies over lavish banquets here.

Serafin and his guards were on the other side of the piazza, at the end of a long arcade and not far from the water. The nearby arcade protected them from the eyes of the traders who had begun setting out their meagre stalls, despite the darkness and the early hour. It was a miracle that there was anything left to trade after so many years under siege.

Serafin briefly thought about trying to run away and jump into the canal. But the guards would be quick on the draw. He wouldn't have got halfway before their bullets hit him. No, he must wait for a better opportunity.

By now he knew why the lion had brought him here and not to the prison courtyard. His guards served the three councillors who were working in secret for the Empire and who had betrayed Venice. They wouldn't want the other members of the Council to know, and a captive delivered to the prison by one of the guardsmen's flying lions would certainly have attracted attention. That was just what the traitors had to avoid, so they were making him go the last part of the journey on foot. He would look like a common criminal who just happened to have been picked up by the guards, particularly since many people would recognise him as a Master Thief of the Guild.

Suppose he were to shout out the truth? Suppose he told everyone they passed, everyone here in the piazza, what he had seen? Then he could . . .

His head was jerked roughly backwards. Hands pushed coarse fabric into his mouth, pulled the edges of the cloth over his nose and chin, and tied the ends of it behind his head. The gag was so tight that it hurt. It tasted far from pleasant too.

So much for his plan. Admittedly it hadn't been very well thought out.

Using the barrels of their rifles, the men pushed him out

of the shadow of the arcade and into the square. There was a curious smell in the air. Perhaps it came from the palace dungeons.

Other people seemed to have noticed the stench too. A couple of traders looked up from their stalls with distaste, sniffed the air and grimaced.

Serafin tried to look at his guards, but when he turned his head to one side a rifle butt struck him in the small of the back. 'Keep your eyes ahead!'

The stalls were arranged in two rows, like a shopping street running from the water towards the Basilica of St Mark. Serafin's path crossed them in the middle of the piazza. He now had a clearer view of some of the men and women setting up their stalls by the light of torches and gas lamps. It must still be more than an hour before sunrise, but they wanted to be ready for customers.

However, Serafin noticed that fewer and fewer of the traders were paying attention to their stalls. Several had clustered together, gesticulating and wrinkling their noses. 'Sulphur,' he heard them say again and again. 'Why sulphur? And why here?'

He must have been mistaken: the smell didn't come from the dungeons.

They passed the second row of stalls and left the shopping street behind them. It was about a hundred metres to a narrow side entrance leading into the Doge's Palace. More guardsmen stood on sentry duty to right and left of this entrance, among them a captain of the guard with the badge of the flying lion on his black uniform. With furrowed brow, he was watching Serafin and his companions approaching.

The voices of the traders behind Serafin's back grew louder, more excited, more confused. Serafin felt as if there were a sudden quivering in the air. His skin began to tingle.

Someone screamed. A single shrill scream, not even particularly loud. The captain of the guard at the gate turned his eyes from Serafin to the middle of the piazza. The stench of sulphur was so strong now that it turned Serafin's stomach. Out of the corner of his eye he saw his guards holding their noses. They were getting a much stronger whiff of the smell than he was. The gag around his mouth and nose saved him from the worst of it.

One of the men suddenly stopped and threw up. Another did the same.

'Wait!' ordered one of the soldiers. After a moment's hesitation, Serafin turned round.

Two of his four guards were bent double, coughing and vomiting all over their shiny boots. A third had his hand in front of his mouth. Only the fourth, the one who had given him the order to wait, was still aiming a rifle at him.

Beyond the guards, Serafin saw the crowd of traders scatter. Some were stumbling around blindly through puddles of vomit. Serafin looked back at the side entrance to the Doge's Palace. The guards were fighting their nausea too. Only the captain still stood upright, holding his nose with one hand. He was alternately breathing through his mouth and shouting orders, but no one was obeying them any more.

Serafin silently thanked his guards for the gag. He too felt sick, but its fabric kept the worst of the sulphurous vapours away from him.

As he was still wondering whether this was the chance he'd been waiting for, a deep rumbling sound was suddenly heard. The ground shook. The rumbling grew louder and rose to become a roll of thunder.

One of the stalls in the middle of the square caught fire. Panic-stricken traders performed a wild St Vitus' dance around the flames. A second wooden stall flared up, then a third. In no time the flames were racing along the row, even where the stalls stood too far apart for the fire to cross the gap of its own accord. There was no wind blowing to fan the flames, yet they kept spreading. The air was still, except for the almost imperceptible quivering that made the hairs on Serafin's forearms stand on end.

The captain of the guard glanced at the turbulent water, his keen eyes searching for enemy gunboats or catapults throwing fiery missiles. There was nothing, no attacker. Serafin followed the captain's eyes and looked up at the sky. Again, he saw only darkness there, none of the imperial Egyptian Barques of the Sun.

The two rows of stalls were now blazing fiercely, like flickering torches casting firelight on the facades of the Doge's Palace and the Basilica of St Mark. The screaming traders didn't even try to put out the fires consuming their wares. Panic-stricken, they retreated left and right to the sides of the piazza.

Serafin took a deep breath – the air was still sulphurous – and then ran for it. He had covered all of ten paces before one of his guards noticed that he'd gone. It was the man who had been the first to throw up, and now he was just wiping his lips with one hand. His other hand held his rifle, and he was waving it wildly in Serafin's direction. His companions now looked up too and saw their prisoner getting away. One of them swung his gun round, took aim and fired. The bullet whistled past Serafin's ear. Before the man could fire his gun again, a new wave of nausea overcame him. Another of the guards fired, but his bullet came nowhere near Serafin. The shot dug a groove in the paved surface of the piazza, far from its target, leaving a golden crater in the flickering firelight.

Serafin ran for all he was worth. He was soon breathless, but he didn't tear off the gag. He raced over to the Basilica of St Mark, and only there did he venture to turn. No one was following him. His guards were thinking only of themselves. One was propping himself on his gun as if it were a crutch. Many of the traders were also crouching on the ground, well away from the flames, their faces buried in their hands. Others had sought shelter behind the columns of the arcade and were staring, dazed, at the blazing inferno consuming their goods.

The thunderous sound came again, this time so loud that they all put their hands over their ears. Serafin took cover behind a tub of flowers, one of many flanking the Basilica. It would have been more sensible to escape and plunge into one of the alleyways, but he couldn't run away now. He had to see what happened next.

At first it looked as if all the burning market stalls were suddenly collapsing into a blazing pyre. Only then did Serafin see the true extent of the disaster.

Among the burning rows of stalls, exactly in line with the path between them, the ground had opened up. The crevice was a hundred or a hundred and twenty paces long, and wide enough to swallow up the stalls on its edge.

Serafin caught his breath. He could think of nothing else, not even flight. The guards had assembled outside the palace gateway and stood there like an angry flock of geese, shouting wildly at one another and waving their weapons about, while their captain was desperately trying to restore order.

Serafin crouched lower behind the tub of flowers, until only his eyes were peering over the edge.

Fire blazed inside the crevice. At first it seemed to burn with a regular flame, then it gradually moved away from both ends towards the centre and coalesced into an intolerably bright ball of radiance.

A figure emerged from the firelight.

It hovered there, upright, with something around its head that at first glance resembled a halo. The sight reminded Serafin of depictions of saints on altarpieces, with hands devoutly crossed on their breasts. But then Serafin saw that this figure had the face of a newborn baby, fleshy and swollen. The halo turned out to be a kind of circular saw blade with teeth as long as Serafin's thumbs; it was set on the back of the strange being's head and seemed to be merged with its skin and bone. The crossed hands were gigantic chicken claws, divided into scaly grey segments. The creature's plump body ended not in legs but in something long and pointed that had damp bandages wrapped around it. It looked like a quivering, reptilian tail, prevented by its wrappings from lashing out uncontrollably. The being's bloated eyelids slid back like slugs to reveal eyeballs as black as pitch. The thick lips opened too, showing teeth filed to sharp points.

'Hell presents its compliments,' said the creature. It sounded like the voice of a child, but louder and more penetrating, and it echoed over the whole piazza.

The guards raised their rifles to take aim, but the envoy from Hell laughed at them. It was now hovering two metres above the fiery crevice, and the flames were still bathing it in bright light. Tiny tongues of fire flickered up and down the bandages of its lower body but did not burn the fabric.

'People of Venice,' cried the envoy, in a voice so loud that it even drowned out the crackling of the fire, 'my masters have an offer to make you.' Green saliva dropped from the corners of its mouth, spread into the folds of its double chin, collected above its throat and dripped down. The heat of the flames made the drops evaporate even as they fell.

'From now on,' it said, making a bow as it gave a sly grin, 'from now on we hope to be your friends.'

Something shook the world.

Only a moment ago, the shoal of mermaids had been drifting quietly through the water, a few metres below the surface. Then came a deafening crash, and a shock wave caught them, scattering them as if an angry god had struck the sea with his fist. Merle saw the gondolas above them tossed back and forth like paper boats; some rammed each other, some broke apart. The next moment, invisible forces tore her away from the two mermaids who had been holding her hands. First she was sucked deeper down, then washed up to the surface again, thrown towards a dense mass of floating wreckage from the gondolas. She opened her eyes wide, saw the sharp keels racing towards her like great black sword blades, and was about to scream . . .

The helmet of solidified water took the impact. An abrupt jolt ran through Merle's body, but the pain was bearable. The water was as turbulent as if a hurricane were raging over the surface. Suddenly a mermaid's hands grasped her waist from behind, swiftly steering her under the gondolas and over to the piles of a landing stage, only a few metres away. The mermaid's expression was tense. It was costing her all her strength to resist the alternate forces of pressure and suction. They reached the moorings, and before Merle could react she was catapulted up above the surface, while the Flowing Queen cried out in her mind, *'Hold on!'*

She flung her arms out and caught one of the slippery piles of the landing stage, slipping a little way down it before her flailing feet found any support. Then she swiftly clambered up on the structure and collapsed on the landing stage, coughing up salt water.

The surface of the water around the moorings here was still rough, but it seemed to be calming down gradually. Merle took off the helmet, saw a hand rising from the waves in farewell, and threw the globe into the water. Delicate fingers closed around the neck opening and drew the helmet down into the depths. Merle saw a shoal of pale bodies shoot away beneath the water.

'I feel something . . .' the Queen began slowly. Then she fell silent again.

Merle turned and looked through her strands of dripping hair at the piazza.

At first all she saw was fire.

Then she saw the figure. Saw it as clearly as if every tiny detail, however dreadful, had burned itself on her retina in a split second.

'. . . hope to be your friends,' she heard the creature say.

She scrambled up on to the land, but there she stopped again. She hesitated. Guardsmen were reluctantly gathering around the hovering creature, well out of its reach, yet close enough for their bullets to hit it.

The envoy of Hell paid no attention to the soldiers, but addressed its audience where they stood behind the columns of the arcades and around the sides of the piazza.

'People of Venice, Hell offers you a pact.' With relish, the creature let its words ring out. The echo distorted its childish voice to a grotesque squeal. 'Your rulers, the councillors of this city, have declined our offer. But hear it for yourselves and make your own decision.' Again there was a pause, interrupted by the commands of the captain of the guard. A second and then a third troop of reinforcements came hurrying up, accompanied by a dozen cavalrymen mounted on stone lions.

'You fear the wrath of the Pharaonic Empire,' continued the envoy, 'and you are right to do so. You have held off the Empire for over thirty years, but soon the Pharaoh's armies of mummies will be preparing for their great attack, and they will sweep you off the face of the earth. Unless . . . unless you have powerful allies on your side. Allies like my master!' A snort made its way between the fleshy lips. 'The armies of our own realm can hold their own against the Egyptians. We could protect you. Yes, we could indeed.'

Merle felt spellbound by the repellent sight of that fiery figure. More and more people were streaming to the sides of the piazza from all directions, attracted by the flames, the noise, and the prospect of an impressive spectacle.

'There's no time to lose,' said the Flowing Queen. *'Come on, run to the Campanile!'*

'But the fire . . .'

'If you skirt around the fire to the left, you can make it. Please, Merle – this is our best chance!'

Merle ran. The tower of the Campanile rose in the angle of the L-shaped piazza. She had to go all the way along the fiery crevice, behind the back of the envoy from Hell, whose face was turned to the Doge's Palace as it hovered above the flames. The stench of sulphur was overpowering. The envoy was still speaking, but Merle hardly heard it. Agreeing to the offer from the Prince of Hell might seem tempting at first – but a mere glance at this nauseating creature showed that if the Venetians made such a pact they would be out of the frying pan, into the fire. True, they might then defeat the Empire and keep the Egyptians away from the lagoon. But what new rulers would move into the palaces of the city to replace the sphinx commanders, and what sacrifices would they demand?

Merle had covered half the distance to the Campanile when she realised that its entrance was not guarded. The men at the gate had joined the troops outside the palace. The muzzles of at least a hundred guns were now aimed at the envoy, and more armed men were arriving every minute. The lions on the ground, all of them wingless granite beasts, were angrily scraping the paving of the piazza with their claws, scoring furrows in it. Their riders had difficulty restraining them.

'One drop of blood from every man, woman and child in the city,' cried the envoy from Hell, addressing the crowd. 'Just one drop from everyone, and the pact is sealed. Citizens of Venice, think well! How much blood will the Empire demand? How many of you will die in the battle for the lagoon, and how many more deaths will the Pharaoh's rule require after that?'

A little boy, seven years old at most, tore himself away from his horrified mother and ran past the soldiers on his short little legs to confront the envoy.

'The Flowing Queen protects us!' he shouted at the creature. 'We don't need your help!'

Panic-stricken, his mother tried to run after him, but others held her fast. She struggled and struck out, but could not free herself. She kept shouting her child's name.

The boy looked up defiantly at the envoy again. 'The Flowing Queen will always protect us!' Then he simply turned and ran back to the others. The envoy did him no harm.

Merle felt a pang at the little boy's words. It took her a moment to realise that the pang had not been her own feeling, but the Flowing Queen's pain, despair and shame.

'*They rely on me*,' she said tonelessly. '*They all rely on me. And I have let them down*.'

'But they don't know what's happened to you.'

'*They'll find out soon enough. At the very latest when the Pharaoh's war galleys drop anchor in the lagoon and the Barques of the Sun rain fire from the sky*.' She fell silent for a moment, and then added, '*They had better accept the envoy's offer.*'

Merle almost fell over her own legs with shock. Only another twenty metres to the tower.

'You don't mean it!' she cried. 'Are you serious?'

'*It's a possibility.*'

'But . . . but Hell! I mean, what do we know about it?' And she quickly added, 'I mean, Professor Burbridge's research in itself is enough for us to wish it – well, to wish it to the Devil.'

'*It's a possibility,*' the Queen repeated. Her tone was unusually flat and weak. The little boy's words seemed to have moved her profoundly.

'A pact with the Devil is never a possibility!' Merle disagreed, gasping for air. Running and arguing at the same time was more than she could manage. 'The old stories show us that. Everyone who ever made a pact with the Devil lost out in the end. Everyone!'

'*Again, those are only stories, Merle. Do you know whether anyone's really ever tried it?*'

Merle looked back over her shoulder at the envoy in the middle of the flames. 'But look at it! And don't go giving me any of those clever sayings about not judging a person by outward appearances! It isn't even a person! It's not human.'

'Nor am I.'

Stumbling, Merle reached the gateway to the Campanile. It was open. 'Listen,' she gasped, exhausted, 'I didn't mean to insult you. But Hell . . .' She broke off and shook her head. 'Perhaps you really aren't human enough to understand.'

With that, she pulled herself together and entered the tower.

As she ran, Merle had passed within a few metres of Serafin's hiding place, but he didn't see her. His eyes were fixed on the envoy. The envoy – and the ever-growing throng of soldiers gathering to face it.

The part of the piazza directly outside the Basilica of St Mark was filling with people too. They had come from all directions to see what was going on. Some might already have heard that an envoy had arrived from Hell, but they probably hadn't believed it. Now they saw the truth with their own eyes.

Serafin was still fighting an urge to run away. He had barely escaped the dungeons, and every minute he spent here made it more likely that he would be recognised and recaptured. It was stupid, just stupid, to hide here behind a tub of flowers while the guards were looking for him!

But at this moment the soldiers had other things on their minds, and Serafin repressed the thought of the danger he was in. He had to find out for himself how this ended; he must hear what the envoy had to say.

And he saw something else: three men had come out of the palace. Three councillors in magnificent robes. Purple and scarlet and gold. The traitors. The councillor in gold went up to the captain of the guard and spoke to him. He was clearly agitated.

The flames flared higher for a moment, caressing the envoy's body with their fiery tongues, throwing light on the smile dividing its flabby features.

'One drop of blood,' it cried. 'Think well, citizens of Venice! Just one drop of blood!'

Merle raced up the steps of the Campanile. Her breath was coming fast. Her heart sounded as if it would burst her ribcage. She couldn't remember when she had last run so hard.

'*What do you know about the Traitor of Old?*' asked the Flowing Queen.

'Only what everyone knows. The old story.'

'He was never a traitor. Or not in the way the story tells it.'

Merle was having difficulty in getting her breath back and talking; even listening was a problem.

'I'll tell you what really happened long ago, when they made Vermithrax into the Traitor of Old,' the Flowing Queen went on. *'But first you ought to know* what *he really is.'*

'And . . . and what . . . is . . . he?' gasped Merle as she ran up the stairs, two at a time.

'Vermithrax is a lion. One of the old ones.'

'A . . . a lion?'

'*A winged, talking lion.*' The Queen stopped for a moment. *'Or at least he was when I last saw him.'*

Merle stopped in surprise. She also had a bad stitch in her side. 'But . . . but lions don't talk!'

'Not the lions you know. But once, long ago, many years before the awakening of the Pharaoh and the age of the War of the Mummies, they could all speak. They flew higher and faster than the greatest sea eagles, and their songs were lovelier than the songs of men and merfolk.'

'So what happened?' Merle started moving again, although all she could do was drag herself wearily on. She was still wet through and completely exhausted and, although she was sweating, she was trembling all over as well.

'The stone lions and the people of Venice had been allies since time immemorial. No one knows how the lions originally came here. Perhaps they were beings from some distant corner of the earth? Or the work of a Venetian alchemist? It makes no difference. The lions served the Venetians, fighting with them in many wars, they accompanied their ships on the dangerous trading routes off the coast of Africa, and they protected the city with their lives. The grateful Venetians soon had the lions' faces on all the emblems and banners of the city, and they were given one of the islands in the north of the lagoon as a home.'

'If the lions were so strong and powerful, why didn't they build a city of their own?' Merle could hardly hear her own words, they passed her lips so faintly.

'Because they trusted the citizens of Venice and felt bound to them. Trust was always strong in their nature. They did not want it any other way. Their bodies might be made of stone, their flight swift and their songs full of poetry, but lions have never been seen to build a house. They had become used to living with human beings, they liked a roof over their heads and the comfort of living in a city. And that, I fear, was their undoing.'

Merle stopped briefly by one of the narrow windows in the tower looking out on the piazza. She was horrified to see how the number of soldiers and guards had increased during the last few minutes. Obviously the councillors had summoned uniformed men from every quarter of the city, ranging from nightwatchmen to much-decorated captains. There must be hundreds of them. And they were all aiming rifles and revolvers or even drawn swords at the envoy from Hell.

'Go on! Hurry up!'

When Merle, sighing, had turned to climb the rest of the steps, the Queen went on with her story. '*No good could come of it. Human beings aren't made to live in peace with other creatures. It turned out as it was bound to. It began with fear. Fear of the lions' strength, of their mighty wings, their fangs, their powerful claws. People came to forget how much the lions had done for them, they forgot that Venice owed its supremacy in the Mediterranean to the lions alone. Fear turned to hatred, and hatred became a determination to make the lions subject to them once and for all – for they would not and could not do without them. On the pretext of holding a banquet for the lions as a token of the gratitude of Venice, they induced them to assemble on their island. Ships carried over countless cattle and pigs, ready butchered. The abattoirs had been given orders to make all their stocks available for the feast. And there was wine from the best vineyards of Italy, and clear spring water from the Alpine rocks. The lions feasted in luxury on their island for two days and two nights, but then, slowly, the sleeping draught which the cunning Venetians had rubbed on the meat and mixed into the wine and water began to work. On the third day, not a lion in the whole lagoon was still on its legs; they were all fast asleep. And now the butchers had to set to work again, this time chopping the wings off the lions!'*

'They . . . they simply . . .'

'Chopped them off. Yes, indeed. The lions felt nothing, the drug in their blood was too strong. Their wounds were treated, and hardly any died of their injuries, but then the Venetians left them behind on the island, in the knowledge that the weakened lions were trapped. Lions are afraid of the water, as you know, and the few who tried to leave the island by swimming were so frightened that they drowned in the waves.'

Merle felt such revulsion that she stood still again. 'Then why are we going to so much trouble to save the city? After all the Venetians have done to the lions and the merfolk! If the Egyptians attack and raze everything to the ground, it's no more than they deserve.'

She sensed that the Queen was smiling gently; it was like a strange, warm feeling in the pit of her stomach. *'Don't sound so bitter, little Merle. You're a Venetian too, like many others who know nothing of this story. The crime against the lions was committed a long time ago, many generations in the past.'*

'And you really think people are any wiser today?' asked Merle scornfully.

'*No. They will probably never be any wiser. But people shouldn't be made to pay for crimes they didn't commit themselves.'*

'So what about the mermaids they harness to their boats? You said yourself they'll all die.'

The Flowing Queen was silent for a moment. '*If more of you knew that, if more people knew the truth . . . perhaps there would be no more such injustices.'*

'You say you're not human yourself – yet you defend us. Where do you get that damned kindness from?'

'*Damned kindness*?' repeated the Queen, amused. '*Only a human being could link those two words in the same sentence. Perhaps that's one of the reasons why I think there's still hope for you. But don't you want to hear the rest of the lions' story? We're nearly at the top of the tower, and by the time we reach it you ought to know about the part Vermithrax played.'*

'Go on.'

'*The lions recovered only slowly, and they argued among themselves, wondering what to do next. It was certain that they were captives on their own island. They were weak, the pain in their shoulders was nearly killing them, and they were in despair. The*

Venetians made them an offer: they would go on having food brought to the island if the lions would serve them as slaves. After much debate, the lions agreed. Some of them were moved to another island, where scientists and alchemists began carrying out experiments on them. New generations of stone lions were bred until they became what they are today – not just animals, but not the equal of their noble ancestors. A race of lions born without wings who have forgotten how to sing.'

'And what about Vermithrax?' asked Merle. 'And the lions who *can* still fly today?'

'*When the Venetians did that treacherous deed, a small group of lions happened to be away from the lagoon, spying out the lands of the east for their human allies. When they came home, they learned what had happened, and they roared with anger. But for all their fury there were too few of them to do more than skirmish with the Venetians. So they decided to leave rather than face certain defeat in fighting a superior power. There were no more than a dozen of them, but they flew all the way south across the Mediterranean and on into the heart of Africa. They lived there for a while among the lions of the savannah, until they realised that those African lions accepted them as their own kind only out of fear. Then the stone lions went on, high into the mountains of the hot countries, and they stayed there a long time. The injustice of the Venetians became a story and then a myth. But finally, about two hundred years ago, a young lion called Vermithrax was born. He believed in the truth of the old legends, and his heart was heavy with grief for the fate of his people. He decided to come back here and revenge himself on the treacherous citizens of Venice. But few lions would join him, for by now the mountains had become the home of the fugitives' descendants, and hardly any of them liked the idea of setting off for the uncertainty of a strange country.*

'So it was that Vermithrax set off for Venice with only a handful of companions. He firmly believed that the enslaved lions of the city would join him and turn on their tormentors. But Vermithrax had made a serious mistake: he had underestimated the power of time.'

'The power of time?' asked Merle, puzzled.

'Yes, Merle. Time had long since healed the wounds and, even worse, it had made the lions docile. Their old love of comfort had mastered the new, mute, flightless breed of lions. They were content with their existence as servants of the Venetians. None of them knew about life in freedom now, and their ancestors' abilities were long forgotten. Few were ready to stake their lives for the sake of a rebellion which was not their own. They would rather obey the orders of their human masters than rise up against them. Vermithrax led an assault on the city which cost many lives and left

large parts of Venice in rubble and ashes, but it was ultimately doomed to fail. His own people turned against him. Lions overcame him, the lions he had wanted to liberate who now, of their own free will, had become the servants of mankind.'

'But then *they* were the real traitors, not Vermithrax!'

'It all depends how you look at it. To the Venetians, Vermithrax was a murderer who had attacked them out of the blue, killing countless people and trying to rouse the stone lions to rebellion. From their point of view, what they did made perfect sense. They killed most of the attackers, but they let a few live so that the scientists could breed a new race of flying lions. No one remembered what it had been like when all the lions still had wings, so it seemed to humans an alluring idea to have lion servants who could carry great weights on their pinions, or, in time of war, attack the enemy from the air, as Vermithrax had when he attacked the city. A small number of these new lions were bred, a cross between the free, winged lions who had come home from Africa and the obedient and docile slaves of Venice. You've seen the result: the flying lions on which the guards of the City Council now ride. You've already met some of them.'

'What about Vermithrax?'

'They thought up a particularly harsh punishment for Vermithrax. Instead of killing him, they imprisoned him in this

tower. He had to suffer captivity up in these airy heights, and nothing is worse for a winged lion than to be unable to fly. It was doubly cruel for Vermithrax, who had flown free for many years over the wide savannahs of Africa. And his spirit was broken too – not by his defeat, but by the treachery of his own kind. He couldn't understand their indifference, their doglike devotion to their masters, or the ease with which they had turned against him at the command of men. The knowledge of that treachery was the worst of all punishments to him, so he decided it was time to put an end to his own life. He refused the food they brought him, not out of fear that it might be poisoned but hoping to die quickly. However, that fierce rebel Vermithrax was probably the first of his race to discover that a creature made of stone needs no nourishment. Even stone lions feel hunger, and in fact eating is one of their favourite occupations – but they don't need food to keep them alive. So Vermithrax lives in this tower today, up at the very top, where he can look out over the city, yet is its prisoner.' The Flowing Queen paused for a moment, and then added, *'To be honest, I don't know what kind of state we shall find him in now.'*

Merle was approaching the last landing on the stairs. Light came in through a window and fell on a heavy steel door. Its surface shimmered with a blue light. 'How did you meet Vermithrax?'

'When he led his companions here from Africa, almost two hundred years ago, he thought he ought to imitate human beings in one thing so that he could be their equal – he must overcome a lion's inborn fear of water. His ancestors had been enslaved because they couldn't face the waters of the lagoon. They had become prisoners on their own island, and Vermithrax didn't want to fall into the same trap. As soon as he saw the lagoon before him, he plucked up his courage and, weary as he was, plunged into the water. But even the bravest of lions could not meet that challenge. The water and the cold paralysed him, and he was in danger of drowning.'

'And you saved him?'

'I read his mind as he sank into the depths. I recognised the boldness of his plan and admired his strength of will. A project like his must not fail before it had even begun. So I told the merfolk to bear him up and back to the surface, and to take him safely to the shore of an uninhabited island. I made myself known to him too, and as he came back to his senses and took new heart, we held long conversations. I won't say we made friends – he understood too little of what I really was for that, and I think he feared me because I –'

'Because you yourself are water?'

'I am the lagoon. I am the water. I am the wellspring in which the merfolk live. But Vermithrax was a hot-headed warrior with

an unshakeable will. He felt respect for me, and gratitude, but he feared me too.'

The Flowing Queen fell silent as the exhausted Merle reached the top of the staircase. The steel door of the tower room was three times her own height and well over a metre wide. Two huge bolts were fixed to the front of it and driven into place.

'How are we going to –' she began, but she was interrupted by the noise out in the piazza which suddenly grew much louder. She quickly ran to the barred window and looked down.

From up here she had a breathtaking view over the front of the piazza, and the fiery crevice that had opened up in the middle of it. For the first time she saw that the crevice ended a few metres from the water. If the cleft had run on into the sea, Merle and the mermaids would have been drawn straight into the flames by the pull of the current.

But it was not this realisation that chilled the blood in her veins. It was the disaster just beginning down below.

Three winged lions swooped down from the roof of the Doge's Palace, urged on by the cries of their riders. The City Council had made its decision. Once and for all, there would be no more negotiations with the Princes of Hell.

Before the envoy could react, the three lions were attacking. Two raced past the envoy to right and left, just missing it, passing through the flames too fast for their riders to be scorched. But the third lion, the one in the middle of the formation, seized the envoy with jaws opened wide, got a grip on the middle of its stout body, snatched it away from the flaming crevice and carried it off. The envoy screamed, making terrible sounds too high and shrill for human ears to bear. The creature was held horizontally in the lion's jaws, its bandaged, reptilian lower body twisting and turning like a fat maggot. All over the piazza people were writhing in pain; even soldiers dropped their weapons and put their hands over their ears.

With the envoy in its mouth, the lion flew over the rooftops in a tight curve. Then it soared at speed towards the soldiers who had gathered outside the palace. When it was above their heads it let the screaming creature drop like a piece of rotten meat.

'*Merle!*' cried the Flowing Queen in her mind. '*Merle, the door!*'

But Merle could not tear her eyes from the spectacle. The soldiers scattered just fast enough for the envoy not to hit them. Screaming, it struck the ground in their midst, its haughty manner all gone now, nothing but a monster, its huge chicken claws flailing the air with nothing to grasp, while the reptilian tail at the end of its body drummed the paving in panic.

'Merle . . .!'

For a few moments silence reigned in the whole piazza. People were struck dumb, forgot to breathe, unable to take in what had happened before their eyes.

Then a shout of triumph arose. The pack had scented blood. No one thought of the consequences now. After almost four decades under siege, in fear of the outside world, their feelings were breaking out.

Words emerged from the shouting, and then a shrill, raging chant: 'Kill the brute! Kill the brute!'

'Merle! We don't have any time!'

'Kill the brute!'

'Please!'

'Kill the brute!'

The gap made by the envoy's fall among the ranks of soldiers closed in a mêlée of bodies pressing forward, flashing blades, distorted faces. Dozens of arms rose and fell, hitting out at the creature on the ground with swords, rifle butts, bare fists. The envoy's screams turned to whimpering, and then died away entirely.

'The door, Merle!'

When Merle turned, as if numbed, her glance fell on the two mighty bolts again. They were so large!

'*You must open it, now,*' begged the Queen.

On the other side of the steel, a lion roared.

THE TRAITOR OF OLD

There was no point in asking questions now. Merle had undertaken a task. She had made her decision when she drank the contents of the flask, or maybe even before that, when she left the party and the lighted lanterns and set off with Serafin. An adventure – well, that was what she'd wanted.

It was surprisingly easy to push back the lower bolt. At first she braced her body against it, but the gigantic steel bolt slid to the left as if it had been oiled only the day before.

The second bolt proved more difficult. It was anchored in the steel a good hand's breadth above Merle's head, too high for her to throw her whole weight against it. It was a long time before she finally managed to shift it slightly. Sweat was streaming down her face. The Flowing Queen was silent.

There – the bolt slid to the left. At last!

'*You must push the two halves of the door in*,' the Flowing

Queen told her. She didn't sound really relieved yet. Soldiers would soon reappear on the scene, and by that time they must have freed Vermithrax.

Merle hesitated for only a split second. Then she leaned both hands against the steel door. It swung in with a metallic, creaking sound.

The tower room in the Campanile was larger than she had expected. In the dark, she could make out a tangle of rafters supporting the top of the tower. Pigeons fluttered in the air far, far above. White droppings covered the floorboards like fine snow, so dry and dusty that Merle sent little clouds of them flying up with every step she took. The stale air was acrid with the smell of the pigeon droppings. The inmate of this attic dungeon, however, had no smell of his own, or none that could be distinguished from that of the stone all around.

The place was very dark. A single ray of light fell through a window halfway between the floor and the lower rafters of the roof of the tower. Outside, the sun was rising at last. Over the window, bars as thick as Merle's thighs sliced the sunlight.

The walls too were covered with a network of steel bars, as if the prisoner's jailers had feared he might otherwise simply tear them down. Even the rafters high up in the roof had bars thrust in among them.

The light coming in through the window fell at a slant through the tower room like a skein of glittering ropes, and came to rest in the centre of the loft. Outside that yellow patch of light, darkness held sway; Merle could not see the opposite wall.

She felt very small and lost under the high arch of the doorway. What am I supposed to do now? she wondered.

'*You must greet him. He must know we come in peace.*'

'He won't recognise you if you don't speak to him yourself,' replied Merle.

'*Oh yes, he will.*'

'Er . . . hello?' Merle said softly.

Pigeons rustled in the rafters.

'Vermithrax?'

There was a clanking sound on the other side of the skein of light. Deep in the darkness.

'Vermithrax? I'm here to –'

She stopped short as the shadows merged to form something solid, physical. A rustling came to her ears, followed by a strong gust like wind – wings unfolding and flexing themselves. Then steps, soft as a cat's paws, not heavy and grating like those of the other lions. An animal's steps, still cautious. Waiting.

'The Flowing Queen is with me,' she managed to say. Very likely Vermithrax would laugh at her.

A shape taller than a horse and twice as broad emerged from the darkness. Next moment, all of a sudden, he was standing in the light, his head bathed in the radiance of the morning sun.

'Vermithrax,' breathed Merle, very quietly.

The Traitor of Old looked at her from proud eyes. Murderous claws shot out of his right forepaw – and were immediately retracted again. A flash of quick death, death a hundred times over. Each of his paws was the size of Merle's head, and his teeth were as long as her fingers. Although his mane was made of stone, it rustled, and with every movement he made it rippled like silky fur.

'Who are you?' His voice was deep, with a slight resonance.

'Merle,' she said unsteadily, and repeated it. 'My name is Merle. I'm one of Arcimboldo's apprentices.'

'And you bear the Flowing Queen with you.'

'Yes.'

Vermithrax took a majestic step towards her. 'You opened the door. Are there soldiers outside, waiting to kill me?'

'They're all in the piazza at the moment, but they'll soon be here. We must hurry.'

He stood still again, and this time his whole body was bathed in the light.

Merle had never seen an obsidian lion before. He was deep black from his nose to his bushy tail. There was a slight lustre on his flanks, his lean back and his leonine face. The hairs of his mighty mane seemed to be in constant movement, rippling almost imperceptibly even when he held his head still. His wings were unfolded in the air above him, each almost three metres long. Now he folded them as if casually, without a sound. She felt that draught of air again.

'Hurry.' Lost in thought, he repeated her last word.

Merle felt impatience rise in her. Lion or no lion, she didn't want to die just because he couldn't make up his mind whether to trust her.

'Yes, hurry,' she said firmly.

'*Give him your hand.*'

'You mean it?'

The Queen did not answer, so Merle, her heart sinking, moved towards the obsidian lion. Motionless, he waited for her. Only when she put out her hand to him did he raise his right forepaw in a smooth movement, bringing it up to rest under Merle's fingers.

All at once a change came over him. His gaze grew softer.

'Flowing Queen,' he murmured, scarcely audibly, and bent his head.

'He can feel you?' asked Merle in her mind

'Stone lions are sensitive creatures. He sensed my presence the moment you opened the door, or you'd be dead by now.'

The lion spoke again, and this time his dark eyes were turned on Merle. It really was *her* he was looking at for the first time. 'And your name is Merle?'

She nodded.

'A beautiful name.'

She wanted to say: This is no time for compliments. But then she just nodded again.

'Do you think you can ride on my back?'

Of course she had guessed this was coming. But now that she faced the immediate prospect of riding a genuine stone lion – and a talking, flying lion at that – her knees felt as weak and vulnerable as air bubbles.

'You needn't be afraid,' said Vermithrax in a strong voice. 'Just hold on tight.'

Hesitantly, she came closer and watched him lie down on the floor.

'*Get on with it*,' the Queen urged her impatiently.

With a silent sigh, Merle swung herself up on the lion's back. To her amazement, the obsidian under her felt warm, and it seemed to fit itself to the shape of her legs. She sat there as securely as if she were in a saddle.

'Where do I hold on?'

'Put your hands deep into my mane,' said Vermithrax, 'and hold on as tight as you can.'

'Won't I hurt you?'

He laughed softly, with a touch of bitterness, but gave no answer. Merle did as he said. The lion's mane did not feel like real hair, but nor did it feel like stone. It was hard yet flexible, like the stems of an underwater plant.

'If it comes to a fight,' said the lion, looking straight at the door, 'get down as low as possible on my neck. On the ground I can try to protect you with my wings.'

'All right.' Merle tried to keep her trembling voice under control, not very successfully.

Vermithrax began to move, prowling like a cat towards the door. Then, quick as a flash, he was through it and on the top landing of the stairway. He carefully judged the breadth of the stairwell, nodded with satisfaction, and spread his wings.

'Couldn't we just walk down the steps?' asked Merle anxiously.

'Hurry, you said.' Before the sound of Vermithrax's words had died away, he had risen gently in the air, glided over the balustrade – and dropped steeply into the depths.

Merle uttered a shrill scream as the wind of their flight pressed her eyes shut and almost catapulted her backwards and off the lion. But then she felt firm pressure in her back – the tip of Vermithrax's tail was pressing her forward into his mane.

Her stomach seemed to turn inside out. They were falling, falling, falling . . . The floor at the bottom of the stairwell filled her whole field of vision as the obsidian lion suddenly returned to horizontal flight, swept on over the floor of the tower, and with a mighty roar shot out through the gate of the Campanile, a bolt of lightning made of black stone, larger, harder and heavier than any cannonball and moving with the force of a hurricane.

'Freeeeeeeeee!' he cried triumphantly into the morning air, which was still heavy with the sulphurous vapours of Hell. 'Free at last!'

It all happened so fast that Merle hardly had time to take in any details, let alone fit them together into a logical sequence of incidents, images and sensations.

People were yelling and running about in confusion. Soldiers spun round. Captains shouted orders. Somewhere a shot rang out, followed by a hail of bullets. One of them bounced off Vermithrax's stone flank like a marble, but Merle herself was not hit.

Flying low, not three metres above the ground, the black obsidian lion swooped across the piazza with her. People scattered, screaming. Mothers seized their children again; they had only just let go of them after the death of the envoy.

Vermithrax uttered a deep growling noise, like rocks falling into the depths of a mine; it was a moment before Merle realised that he was laughing. He moved with astonishing grace, as if he had never been held captive in the Campanile. His wings were not stiff but powerful and supple; his eyes were not blind but keen as a hawk's; his legs were not lame, his claws were not blunt and his mind was not clouded.

'*He has lost faith in his people*,' the Flowing Queen explained in Merle's thoughts, '*but not in himself*.'

'You said he wanted to die.'

'That was a long time ago.'

'I want to live, live, live,' roared the obsidian lion, as if he too had heard the Queen's words . . .

'Did he?'

'No,' said the Queen, *'but he can sense me, and perhaps sometimes he can sense what I'm thinking too.'*

'What *I* am thinking!'

'What we *are thinking.'*

Vermithrax soared over the crevice leading down to Hell. The flames were out, but a wall of grey smoke divided the piazza like a curtain. Merle could vaguely see that stones and rubble were rising into the crevice from below, gradually sealing it again. Soon only the paving stones that had been torn up would betray what had happened there.

More bullets whistled around Merle's ears but, strangely enough, all through the flight she had no fear of being hit. Everything was happening much too fast.

She looked to her left, and saw the three traitors standing with the guards in the middle of a puddle of slimy fluids that were flowing from the envoy's body.

Purple. Gold. And scarlet. The councillors had seen who was riding on the lion's back. And they knew that Merle knew their secret.

She looked ahead of her again, and the piazza was left behind as waves rippled away below her. The water glowed golden in the light of dawn, promising them a way to freedom. To their right was the Giudecca. Next moment they had left its rooftops and turrets behind too.

Merle let out a shrill cry, not of fear this time, just to give vent to her feelings, a cry of euphoria and relief. The cool wind sang in her ears. At last she could breathe deeply again, and it did her good after the dreadful smell of sulphur in the piazza. Wind blew through her dress, her skin, her bones. Wind caressed her hair, flowed through her eyes, through her mind. She was one with the air, she was one with Vermithrax as he carried her over the sea, ten or fifteen metres above its waves of liquid fire. Everything was bathed in red and yellow, herself too. Only the obsidian body of Vermithrax remained black as the night racing away from day.

'Where are we going?' Merle tried to shout above the roar of the wind, but she wasn't sure that she had succeeded.

'Away,' cried Vermithrax in the best of high spirits. 'Away, away, away!'

'*The circle of besiegers*,' the Flowing Queen reminded Merle. '*Remember the Egyptian reconnaissance craft and the Barques of the Sun*.'

Merle repeated what she had said for the lion's benefit. As she did so, it struck her that Vermithrax had been imprisoned in the Campanile so long that he could know nothing at all about the rise of the Empire and the Pharaoh's war of annihilation.

'There's a war going on,' she explained. 'It's war all over the world. Venice is under siege by the Egyptian army.'

'Egyptian?' marvelled Vermithrax.

'The army of the Pharaonic Empire. It's besieging the lagoon. We'll never get through it without a plan.'

Vermithrax laughed aloud. 'But I can fly, little girl!'

'So can the imperial Barques of the Sun,' replied Merle, her cheeks flushed red. Little girl, indeed! Huh!

Vermithrax swerved slightly, and looked over his shoulder. 'You make your plan. I'll deal with our friends back there!'

Merle looked back too, and saw that half a dozen flying lions were pursuing them, ridden by black figures clad in leather and steel.

'The guard! Can you shake them off?'

'We'll see.'

'Don't do anything reckless!'

The lion laughed again. 'We're going to get on well together, brave little Merle.'

She had no time to find out whether he was making fun of her, for a shrill hiss came to her ears – rifle bullets rushing past them.

'They're firing at us!'

Their pursuers were about a hundred metres behind. Six lions, six armed men in the pay of the traitors.

'Bullets can't hurt me,' cried Vermithrax.

'Well, that's just great! Maybe not. They can hurt *me*, though!'

'I know. That's why we're going to . . .' He broke off and gave his booming laugh. 'No, I'll let it be a surprise.'

'He's crazy!' If Merle had spoken out loud, it would have been in tones of resignation.

'Just a little crazy, maybe.'

'Do you think I'm crazy?' asked the obsidian lion, amused.

Why pretend? 'You were kept prisoner in that tower too long. And you don't know anything about us human beings.'

'Didn't you say the same to me?' the Flowing Queen put in. *'Don't make it too easy for yourself.'*

Vermithrax made a sharp turn to the right to avoid another burst of fire. Merle swayed on his back, but again the bushy tip of his tail pressed her firmly towards his mane.

'If they go on firing at random like this, they'll soon run

out of ammunition,' she shouted into the headwind.

'Those are only warning shots. They want us alive.'

'What makes you so sure?'

'They could have hit you long ago if they'd wanted to.'

'Does Vermithrax know that?'

'Of course. Never underestimate his intelligence. These flying manoeuvres are harmless fun. He's enjoying himself. He probably just wants to find out if he's forgotten anything over all these years.'

Merle's stomach felt as if hands were pulling it several different ways. 'I feel sick.'

'It will pass over,' said Vermithrax.

'It's all very well for you to talk.'

The lion looked back. 'There they are.'

He had let their pursuers catch up. Four were still behind them, but now two were flanking them, one on each side. One of the riders, a white-haired captain, looked Merle in the eye. He was riding a quartz lion.

'Surrender!' he shouted over the gap between them. He was about ten metres away. 'We are armed, and we outnumber you. If you fly on in that direction, you'll fall into Egyptian hands. We cannot allow that – and you can't want it either.'

'Which councillor do you serve?' Merle called back.

'Councillor Damiani.'

'*Not one of the three traitors*,' said the Queen.

'Why are you pursuing us?'

'I have my orders. And for God's sake, girl, the creature you're riding is the Traitor of Old – the creature who left half Venice in dust and ashes. You can't expect us simply to let him go.'

Vermithrax turned his head to the captain and scrutinised him with his black obsidian eyes. 'If you give up and turn back now, I will let you live, man.'

Now a strange thing happened. It was the reaction not of the captain but of his lion that startled Merle. Vermithrax's words had roused the winged animal from the indifference with which its kind usually obeyed the orders of their human masters. The lion stared at Vermithrax, and for a moment its wings beat faster. The captain also noticed, and tugged at the reins in annoyance. His lips formed the words, 'Easy there!' although the wind blew the sound of them away.

'*It's because Vermithrax is talking, that's what the lion can't understand*,' explained the Flowing Queen.

'Speak to it,' Merle called into the obsidian lion's ear. 'It's our best chance.'

Vermithrax abruptly dropped ten metres down through

the air. His paws were now only the height of two men above the rough sea. The closer they came to the waves, the more aware Merle became of their speed.

'Now!' roared Vermithrax. 'Hold very tight!'

Merle buried her hands still deeper in the obsidian lion's windblown mane as he accelerated with a series of swift wingbeats, then turned at an angle of a hundred and eighty degrees, rose again at once, and suddenly swooped towards their astonished pursuers.

'Lions!' he cried in a voice that carried across the water like thunder. 'Listen to me!'

The six winged lions of the guard hesitated. Their wingbeats slowed. They were now hovering almost motionless, their hind legs dropping so that they had shifted from a horizontal to an almost vertical position in the air. Girths and buckles grated as the six riders were jerked upwards in their safety harness. None of them had expected this manoeuvre; the lions had performed it of their own accord, and the guardsmen were not used to such things.

The captain called to his men to raise their guns. 'Take aim at the girl!' But in this position the great skulls of their lions were in the soldiers' way, and they were unable to take aim with one hand while holding on to a lion's mane with the other.

'Listen to me!' cried Vermithrax again, looking from lion to lion. He too was hovering on the spot, wings beating gently up and down. 'I once returned to your city to free you from the yoke of your oppressors. To free you for a life at liberty. For a life without compulsion and orders and battles that were never your own. A life with all the air you could wish for beneath your wings! Hunting and fighting and, yes, speaking again if you would like to. A life such as your ancestors lived!'

'*He's using your language*,' the Flowing Queen said to Merle. '*The lions have forgotten their own.*'

'They're listening to him.'

'*Yes, but for how long?*'

The six riders shouted helplessly at their lions, but the voice of Vermithrax drowned them out with ease. 'You hesitate because you have never heard a lion speaking human language before. But do you also hesitate because a lion is ready to fight for his freedom? Look at me, and ask: do you not recognise yourselves in me?'

One of the lions gave a sharp snarl. A barely perceptible quiver ran through Vermithrax.

'He's sad,' the Queen explained, *'because they could be like him, but now they're only animals.'*

Other lions joined in the snarling, and the captain, who had grown up with the voices of lions in his ears and had spent his whole life with them, smiled in the certainty of victory.

'Rise against your masters!' roared Vermithrax angrily. The lions' mood was changing from moment to moment, although Merle did not understand why. 'Refuse to take orders any longer! Throw your riders into the sea or carry them back to the city, but let us go in peace.'

The lion who had snarled first menacingly shot the claws out from its forepaws.

'There's no point in it,' sighed the Flowing Queen. *'It was worth trying, but it's useless.'*

'I don't understand,' said Merle in her mind, confused. 'Why won't they listen to him?'

'They're afraid of him. They fear his superior nature. It's many, many years since any Venetian lion could speak. These lions grew up believing that they themselves are superior to all other lions because of their wings. And now here's a lion even more powerful than they are. They can't make it out.'

Merle felt anger rise in her. 'Then they're just like us humans.'

'*Yes, indeed,*' replied the Queen, with a smile in her voice. '*Does the mirror-maker's apprentice see her own reflection in the glass?*'

'That's right, laugh at me.'

'*I'm sorry. I didn't mean to.*'

Vermithrax spoke softly over his shoulder. 'We shall have to escape. Get ready.'

Merle nodded. Her glance moved over the six guardsmen. None of them had yet managed to aim his gun. But that would change as soon as the lions dropped back into a horizontal position and flew on.

'Ready? We're off!' roared Vermithrax.

What happened next was over so quickly that only later did Merle realise how close to death she had come.

Roaring and beating his wings powerfully, Vermithrax flew forward, underneath and past the formation of the six guardsmen, then rose steeply, turned a somersault in the air over them, and soared away, leaving them behind.

Merle gasped with fear. Even the Queen cried out.

Vermithrax turned once more, and now Merle was on top of him again, clinging to his mane and still not sure how she had survived the last few seconds. The moment when the sea had suddenly been over her instead of under her had been brief, and not really dangerous – Vermithrax was too fast and had worked up too much momentum for Merle to lose her grip. All the same . . . he might at least have warned her!

Once again they were flying fast and low over the surface of the water, this time going south, where the islands of the lagoon were not as many or as small as the islands further north. This meant that they were voluntarily rejecting a whole series of good hiding places, and Merle fervently hoped that Vermithrax had made the right decision. I expect he has a plan, she told herself.

'*I don't think so*,' said the Queen tartly.

'You don't?' Merle did not put her question out loud.

'*No. He doesn't know his way around.*'

'How reassuring.'

'*You must tell him what to do.*'

'Me?'

'*Who else?*'

'So you can say it was all my fault if we land in the middle of nowhere?'

'*Merle, this venture depends on you, not on Vermithrax. Not even on me. It's your own path you are treading.*'

'Even if I don't know what we're going to do?'

'You know already. First, leave Venice. Next, find allies to help us defeat the Empire.'

'Where?'

'What happened in the piazza was at least the first spark, you might say. Perhaps we can fan the flames into a blaze.'

Merle made a face. 'Would you mind putting it a little more clearly?'

'The Princes of Hell, Merle. They've offered to help us.'

Merle felt the ground beneath her dropping away again, although Vermithrax was flying straight ahead towards the horizon.

'You really want to ask Hell for help?' she asked, horrified.

'There's no alternative.'

'What about the Tsarist Empire? People say they stood up to the Pharaoh's troops there too.'

'The Tsarist Empire is under the protection of Baba Yaga. I don't know that it's a good idea to ask a goddess for help.'

'Baba Yaga's not a goddess, she's a witch.'

'In her case I'm afraid it comes to the same thing.'

But before they could pursue this subject any further, Vermithrax issued a warning. 'Careful! This will be uncomfortable!'

Merle glanced swiftly back over her shoulder. Through the black plumage of Vermithrax's wings she saw a lion below them, jaws open and claws outstretched. It was approaching from behind, and this time she, not Vermithrax, was its target!

'If they must do it this way,' growled the obsidian lion sadly. He spun round in mid-flight, so that Merle had to cling on with all her might again. She saw the attacking lion's eyes open wide in an animal reflection of its rider's – then Vermithrax dived down beneath his adversary's paws, made a half-turn, and slit the lion's belly open with a well-judged blow of his own claws. When Merle looked round again, both lion and rider had disappeared. The water of the lagoon was tinged with red.

'They bleed!'

'They may be made of stone, but that doesn't mean they're different from other living creatures inside,' said the Queen. *'Death is dirty and it stinks.'*

Merle quickly turned her eyes away from the red foam on the waves, and once more looked ahead at the few islands in sight. Beyond them, a dark streak on the horizon, lay the mainland.

Two more lions soon caught up. Vermithrax killed one as

swiftly and mercilessly as his first opponent. But the other lion learned from its companion's carelessness, swerved away from the obsidian claws as they lashed out, and tried to attack Vermithrax from below. Vermithrax bellowed as one claw grazed him. At the last moment he escaped the deadly blow. Roaring with anger, he flew in an arc and then raced straight towards his astonished enemy, coming closer, closer, closer. He did not swerve or give way, but soared upward at the very last minute and caught the other lion in the face with his hind paws. Stone shattered, and then both lion and rider were gone.

Merle felt tears on her cheeks. She didn't want this killing, yet there was no way she could stop it. Vermithrax had asked the lions of the guard to let them go. Now he could only defend their lives, and he was fighting with all the strength and resolution of his people.

'*Three more*,' said the Flowing Queen.

'Must they all die?'

'*Not if they surrender*.'

'They won't. You know they won't.'

The captain of the guard was riding one of the three surviving lions. His white hair was blowing in the wind, his face betrayed insecurity. It was up to him to give the word to retreat, but Merle could see that he wasn't even contemplating the idea. Find and capture, those were his orders. Kill if need be. He saw no alternative.

It was quick. Their opponents didn't have the ghost of a chance. The captain was the last left, and once again Vermithrax offered him the chance to retreat. But the soldier only urged his lion on in a louder voice, racing like the wind towards Vermithrax and Merle. Briefly, it seemed as if the lion of the guard might actually land a blow with its claws, but Vermithrax went into an evasive move that had Merle lying at a dangerous diagonal angle again. At the same time, he prepared to counter-attack. His enemy's eyes showed that it understood, but not even the certainty of defeat was enough to make the captain turn and flee. Vermithrax uttered a cry of sorrow as he rammed his claws into the other lion's flank, and then he turned swiftly, so as not to see both rider and mount fall into the water.

For a long time no one said a word. Even the Flowing Queen was silent in her distress.

Islands passed by below them, places where the ruins of old fortifications still stood, former defences against the Empire. Today they were no more than skeletons of stone and steel. The gun barrels of cannon rusted away in the sun;

the salt wind of the Mediterranean had covered them with white crystals. Here and there abandoned tent poles rose from the wilderness of swampland, scarcely to be distinguished from the tall reeds.

Once they flew over a place where the water looked brighter, as if there were white sandbanks below the surface.

'*A submerged island*,' said the Queen. '*The current carried away the walls keeping back the sea long ago.*'

'I know,' said Merle. 'Sometimes you can still hear its bells ringing.'

But even the ghosts were silent today. Merle heard nothing but the wind and the quiet beating of the lion's obsidian wings.

BARQUES OF THE SUN

The morning sun was not strong enough to cast light on the Outcasts' Canal. Its golden light flooded the upper storeys of the houses, but came to an abrupt end eight metres above ground level. Eternal twilight reigned below.

The solitary figure hurrying from doorway to doorway was glad of that. It was in flight, and the dim light was very welcome.

Serafin stole past the facades of the empty buildings, casting frequent glances behind him at the mouth of the next canal. If anyone had followed him, that was where the pursuer would first appear. Or up in the sky on a winged lion, although Serafin thought that unlikely. After all that had happened in the Piazza San Marco, the City Guard probably had more important things to do – hunting Merle down, for instance.

He had recognised her on the back of the black beast that came roaring like a tempest out of the gate of the

Campanile. At first he couldn't believe his eyes, but then he was quite sure. It was Merle, without a doubt. But why was she riding a winged lion, and the biggest Serafin had ever seen at that? The one possible explanation was the Flowing Queen. He could only hope that nothing happened to Merle. It was his fault that she had become involved in all this. Why did he have to keep interfering with things that were none of his business? If they hadn't followed the lion to the house where the traitors met the envoy . . . yes, what then? Perhaps the Pharaoh's galleys would already be moored at the Zattere quay, and the deadly fire of the Barques of the Sun would be reflected in the canals.

In the panic and confusion in the piazza, he had found it easy to slip away down an alley. But it wouldn't be long before the guard found out that Serafin, formerly a Master Thief of the Guild, lived in Umberto's house. The soldiers would be looking for him at the Outcasts' Canal by that afternoon at the latest.

But where else was he to turn? Umberto would throw him out when he heard what had happened. However, Serafin remembered what Merle had said about Arcimboldo. Unlike Umberto, the mirror-maker seemed to be an indulgent master – although, after all the tricks they'd played on him, Arcimboldo probably wouldn't look too kindly on a weaver's apprentice. Still, Serafin decided to risk it.

The boat which Arcimboldo used to deliver new mirrors to his customers once a month was tied up outside the door of the mirror-making workshop. No one knew exactly who those customers were. But who cared about a few magic mirrors? Suddenly Serafin felt none of it was important.

The door of the house was open. Serafin could hear voices inside. He hesitated. He couldn't just walk in. If he came across Dario or one of the other boys, that would be the end of any secrecy. Somehow he had to get the mirror-maker on his own.

He had an idea. He looked attentively at the weaver's workshop on the opposite bank. No one in sight behind its windows. Good. And not a soul in sight outside Arcimboldo's house at the moment either.

Serafin left the shadows of the house entrance where he was hiding, and he ran. He swiftly approached the boat. It was a long, shallow vessel. Over a dozen mirrors hung at the back of the boat in a wooden framework structure; the small spaces between the mirrors were padded with quilted cotton fabric.

More quilts lay in a large heap in the bows of the boat. Serafin pushed a couple aside, crouched down under them and pulled them over his head. With a little luck no one would notice him. He would reveal himself to Arcimboldo when they were under way.

It was a few minutes before he heard voices again. He could make out Dario's voice, muted by the quilts. The boys were putting a last consignment of mirrors on the boat. They fixed them securely in the frame that held them in place and then went back on land. Arcimboldo issued a few instructions, then the rocking of the boat became more marked, and finally it began to move.

Soon afterwards Serafin peered out from under the quilts. The mirror-maker was standing at the other end of the boat, pushing an oar into the water like a gondolier. The craft glided smoothly down the canal, turned a corner, went on. Now and then Serafin heard the traditional warning cries uttered by gondoliers as they approached junctions. But most of the time, silence reigned. Nowhere in the whole city was it as peaceful as on the side canals, deeply embedded as they were in the labyrinthine alleys of this melancholy quarter.

Serafin was biding his time. First he wanted to see where Arcimboldo would land. The gentle rocking of the boat was so soothing, it made him feel drowsy . . .

He woke with a start. He had nodded off. No wonder, under the warm quilts and after a night when he hadn't slept a wink. The rumbling of his stomach had woken him.

When he raised the quilts slightly and peered out, he was greatly surprised: they had left the city and were gliding over open water. Venice was already some way behind them. They were going north towards a group of tiny, marshy islands. Arcimboldo still stood at his oar, looking out to sea with his features fixed like stone.

This was a good opportunity. Out here no one would see them together. On the other hand, Serafin's curiosity was stronger now. Where was Arcimboldo taking the mirrors? No one had lived here since the war began; the outer islands were deserted. Umberto had suspected that Arcimboldo sold his wares to wealthy society ladies, just as the master weaver himself did – but in this wilderness? They had left even the lions' island well behind them. Only the wind blew over greenish-brown waves, and sometimes a fish came into sight.

It was about another half-hour before a tiny island appeared ahead. The mirror-maker was steering for its shore. Far away, high above the mainland, Serafin thought he saw faint streaks in the sky. The Pharaoh's reconnaissance airships: Barques of the Sun, powered by the high priests' black magic. But they were too far off to be a danger to the boat. No barque ventured as far as this into the realm of the Flowing Queen.

The island had a diameter of perhaps two hundred metres, and was overgrown with reeds and shrub-like trees. The wind had pressed the treetops and tangled branches pitilessly down to the ground. Such islands had once been popular sites for the remote villas built by the nobility of Venice. But no one had come here for over thirty years, certainly not to live on the islands. They were splinters of no man's land, ruled only by the foaming sea.

Ahead of the boat, Serafin saw the mouth of a small waterway winding out of the interior of the island. Trees stood close to each other on both banks, their branches touching the water. A great many birds sat among the branches. Once, when Arcimboldo thrust his oar a little too hard into the water, gulls flew up from the undergrowth and fluttered above the treetops in panic.

After one last bend, the waterway led them to a small lake at the heart of the island. Serafin would have liked to lean forward and see how deep the water was, but the risk was too great. Arcimboldo might be lost in thought, but he was certainly not blind.

The mirror-maker let the keel of the boat run gently aground. The hull scraped on sand. Arcimboldo put down the oar and stepped on to the land.

Serafin raised himself just far enough to look over the rail and see the shore of the lake. The mirror-maker was crouching down by a dense thicket, tracing something in the sand with his forefinger. Then he rose, parted the undergrowth with his hands, and disappeared into it.

Quick as a flash, Serafin threw off the quilts and left the boat. He avoided stepping on the strange sign left in the sand by Arcimboldo's fingers, and plunged into the moist twilight that hung over the plants. He could still see Arcimboldo, a vague outline among the leaves and branches.

After a few more steps he saw where the mirror-maker was going. The ruins of a building rose from a clearing. To all appearances, it had once been some Venetian nobleman's summer residence. Nothing now stood of it but the lower parts of the walls, blackened by the soot of a fire that had reduced the place to ashes long ago. The plants had soon begun to reclaim their kingdom: tendrils fanned out as they clambered up the stones, grass grew on the jagged tops of the walls, and a tree leaned out of a hole that had once been a window, looking like a skeleton with bony arms outstretched in greeting.

Arcimboldo approached the ruin and disappeared inside it. Serafin hesitated, then hurried out of hiding and got into cover behind a wall. Bending low, he stole along to one of the burned-out windows. He raised his head cautiously until he could just see over the sill.

The interior of the ruin was a confused maze where the remaining walls were no higher than a man's hip. Large quantities of masonry had been demolished, and several walls had collapsed entirely. The old bricks formed mounds where rampant weeds grew. Surely no normal fire was strong enough to have caused such devastation. This looked more like the aftermath of an explosion.

Arcimboldo walked through the ruin, looking attentively around him. Serafin did not like the idea that there might be other people on this island. Suppose they saw him? They might leave him marooned here, far from all the boat routes to the centre of the lagoon.

Arcimboldo bent down and again traced something on the ground with his finger. As he did so, he turned round on the spot until the signs in the dust formed a circle. Only then did he rise again, turning to look at the centre of the ruins.

'Talamar!' he cried.

Serafin didn't know the word. Perhaps it was a name.

'Talamar!' repeated Arcimboldo. 'The wish is granted, the spell cast, the pact fulfilled.' It sounded like a formula or a magic charm. Serafin was quivering with excitement and curiosity.

Then he noticed the smell of sulphur.

'Talamar!'

The stench was blowing from the ruins. It came from a place hidden behind the blackened remnants of walls.

There was a hissing sound. Serafin moved quietly along the outer wall until he reached a window from which he had a better view of the source of the stench.

It was a hole in the ground, rather like a well. The rim was irregularly raised, suggesting the rim of a crater. This must be the site of the explosion that had destroyed the building. Serafin couldn't see how far down into the ground the opening went. The hissing grew louder. Something was coming closer.

Arcimboldo bowed. 'Talamar,' he said again, not a summons this time but a respectful greeting.

A thin, spindly creature crawled out of the hole on long legs. It was approximately human in form, but its joints seemed to be at the wrong angles, giving it a deformed and sickly look. It moved on all fours, with its stomach upwards, like a child playing at making a bridge out of its body. As a result, its face was on top of its head. The creature was bald and blind. A wreath of iron thorns lay close around its head at eye level, like a bandage. A single thorny spray had come loose and ran across the creature's face, right over its toothless mouth. Where the thorns touched its lips they had left broad swellings like scars.

'Mirror-maker,' whispered the creature named Talamar, repeating Arcimboldo's words. 'The wish is granted, the spell cast, the pact fulfilled. At the service of the dark for ever more.' So saying, it threw a bag of clinking coins into the circle at Arcimboldo's feet.

'At the service of the dark for ever more,' repeated the mirror-maker. That was evidently the end of the ceremony of greeting. 'I have brought the delivery. Thirteen mirrors, made to your master's wishes.'

'Which are also yours, mirror-maker.' In spite of its indistinct utterance, the creature's voice sounded sly. Talamar turned with a complex movement of those angular limbs until its head was dangling over the edge of the opening. It uttered a series of shrill sounds. Quick as lightning a crowd of black creatures swarmed out of the sulphurous shaft, none of them bigger than a baby monkey. They were blind like Talamar, their eye sockets empty. They scurried off, and Serafin soon heard them busy about the boat.

'I have bad news,' said Arcimboldo, without stepping out of the circle. 'The Flowing Queen has left the lagoon. The water has lost its power. I can make no more mirrors until she returns.'

'No more mirrors?' screeched the creature called Talamar, waving one of its thin arms. 'What nonsense is this, old man?'

Arcimboldo remained calm, showing no fear or uneasiness at all. 'You heard me, Talamar. Without the Flowing Queen in the water of the lagoon I cannot make magic mirrors. The most important element is missing. That means no more deliveries.' He sighed, the first sign of emotion he had shown in front of the creature. 'It will probably make no difference, if the Empire captures the city.'

'My masters offered you help,' whispered Talamar. 'But you killed our envoy and rejected our support. The responsibility is yours.'

'Not ours. The responsibility of those who rule us.' There

was scorn in Arcimboldo's voice. 'Those accursed councillors.'

'Councillors! Drivel! Nonsense!' The thing called Talamar was gesticulating wildly, with movements that made it look even weirder and more alarming; it was still standing upside down on all fours. Only now did Serafin see that the creature's heart beat inside a little glass casket fastened to its belly with straps – a gnarled, black muscle like a pulsating heap of excrement. 'Drivel! Drivel!' Talamar continued raging. 'We must have mirrors, more mirrors, more mirrors! It is my master's wish.'

Arcimboldo frowned. 'Tell him that I'm happy to do business with him. Lord Light has always been a good customer.' He said this in a cynical undertone that Serafin picked up clearly; but Talamar ignored it. 'However, with the Flowing Queen gone I can't make mirrors. Besides, the Egyptians will close my workshop – assuming they leave one stone standing on top of another.'

Talamar was still extremely agitated. 'He won't like this. Won't like it at all.'

'Do you fear your master's anger, Talamar?'

'Nonsense, nonsense! Talamar fears nothing. But you should fear it, mirror-maker! You should fear Talamar! And the wrath of Lord Light!'

'There's nothing I can do about it. I did business with you so that the workshop would survive. Without your gold I'd have had to close it long ago. And then what would have become of the children?' The old man shook his head sorrowfully. 'I couldn't allow that.'

'Children, children, children!' Talamar made a scornful gesture. But then the creature's sore lips distorted into a grin. The steely tendril over its mouth stretched taut, pulling the wreath above its eyes tighter. 'What about the children? You have done all you were told to do, I hope?'

Arcimboldo nodded. 'I took the two girls into my house as your master wished.' He hesitated. Serafin could see that he was thinking of saying more, but then decided to keep Merle's disappearance to himself.

Talamar's head swung back and forth. 'You have fulfilled all the Master's wishes?'

'Yes.'

'And they are the right girls?'

'All has been done to Lord Light's satisfaction.'

'How can you know that? You have never met him.'

'If it had been otherwise you'd have told me, I am sure, Talamar.' Arcimboldo grimaced. 'I suspect it would give you particular pleasure to see me fall out of favour with Lord Light.'

The creature uttered a cackling laugh. 'You can supply no more mirrors. The Master will be very angry.' Talamar thought briefly, then made a horrible, distorted face. 'In compensation we will take something else. Earlier than planned.'

Hard as Arcimboldo was trying to show no weakness before Talamar, he could not hide his horror now. 'No! It is too soon. The plan –'

'Has been changed. With immediate effect.'

'That's outside your authority!'

The creature approached Arcimboldo until its thin fingers were almost touching the circle of signs. 'My authority is Lord Light's! You have no right to question it, man! You will obey, that is all.'

Suddenly Arcimboldo's voice sounded unsteady. 'You want the girl?'

Talamar chuckled. 'The girl with mirror-glass eyes. She is ours. You knew it from the first.'

'But she was to have stayed here with us for years!'

'The transformation has begun. That must suffice. Lord Light himself will take care of her.'

'But –'

'Remember, old man: at the service of the dark for ever more! You have sworn an oath. The wish must be granted, the spell cast, the pact fulfilled. You break the pact if you bring us no mirrors. So we will take the girl. And remember, sooner or later she would have been ours anyway.'

'Junipa is only a child!'

'She is the mirror-maiden. You made her so. And as for the other one –'

'Merle.'

'There is great strength in her. A strong will. But not as much power as in the other one. So bring us the mirror-girl, old man. Your creature and soon ours.'

Arcimboldo's shoulders sagged. His eyes were fixed on the ground. He was beaten; defeat was inevitable. In spite of all he had overheard, Serafin felt sorry for him.

The column of black monkey-like creatures came back in groups of three, each trio carrying a mirror overhead; it looked as if they were carrying fragments of the blue sky over the island. They marched into the hole in turn, and then along a pathway winding down the walls of the shaft like the thread of a screw. Soon all the mirrors were out of sight. Once again Arcimboldo and Talamar stood alone on the edge of the way down to Hell.

'At the service of the dark for ever more,' insisted the creature.

'For ever more,' the mirror-maker whispered sadly.

'I will wait for you here to take the mirror-maiden. She is the most important part of the Great Plan. Do not disappoint us, old man.'

Arcimboldo gave no answer. In silence, he watched Talamar go back into the hole on angular limbs, like a human spider. Seconds later, the creature was gone.

The mirror-maker picked up the bag of coins from the ground and set off on the way back.

Serafin was waiting for him in the boat.

'Ah. Did you overhear all that?' Arcimboldo felt too faint to show any real surprise. There was weariness in his movements and voice, dull sadness in his eyes.

Serafin nodded.

'Well – and what do you think of me now?'

'I think you are a desperate man, Master Mirror-Maker.'

'Merle told me about you. You're a good boy. If you knew the whole truth, perhaps you would understand me.'

'Tell me, then.'

Arcimboldo hesitated, and then he got into the boat. 'Perhaps I should.' He passed Serafin, flung the bag of gold carelessly down on the planks and picked up the oar. With weary thrusts, he manoeuvred the boat along the waterway towards the open sea.

Serafin sat down among the empty structures where the mirrors had hung. The wood was covered with small, wet footprints.

'Are you going to do it? Let them have Junipa, I mean?'

'It's the only way. There is far more than my life at stake.' He sadly shook his head. 'The only way,' he repeated dully.

'What will you tell Junipa? The truth?'

'I shall tell her she is one of the Chosen, and always was. Just like Merle – only in a very different way.'

Serafin took a deep breath. 'You really do have a great deal to tell me, Master Mirror-Maker.'

Arcimboldo held his gaze for a few seconds, and then he looked out at the lagoon, far away over it, further than the landscape, further than this world.

A seagull settled on the rail beside Serafin and looked at him with dark eyes.

'It has turned cool,' said the mirror-maker softly.

At some point Merle remembered her mirror again. The mirror in the pocket of her dress. As she held on to the lion's mane with one hand she took it out with the other. It had survived their flight from Venice intact. The surface of the water mirror shone silvery in the afternoon light, lapping gently back and forth, never spilling a single drop out of the frame. Once a misty flicker passed over it, only briefly, and then it was gone again. The phantom. Perhaps a being from another world, another Venice. What was that other Venice like? Were its people as afraid of the Pharaoh's Empire as the Venetians in this world? Did the Barques of the Sun hover like hungry birds of prey in its sky too? And was there another Merle there, a Serafin, a Flowing Queen?

'*Perhaps*,' said the familiar voice in her head. '*Who knows?*'

'Well, who should know if you don't?'

'*I am only the lagoon.*'

'You know so much.'

'*Yet I have no knowledge going beyond the bounds of this world.*'

'Is that true?'

'*Certainly*.'

Vermithrax spoke. His resonant voice drowned out the rushing of his wingbeats. 'Is it her you're talking to? The Queen?'

'Yes.'

'What does she say?'

'She says you're the bravest lion the world has ever seen.'

Vermithrax purred like a domestic cat. 'Extremely kind of her. But you don't have to flatter me, Merle. I owe you my freedom.'

'You don't owe me anything,' she sighed, suddenly downcast. 'But for you I might well be dead.'

She put the water mirror back in the pocket of her dress and carefully did up the button. A part of another world, she thought, bemused. So close to me. Perhaps what Serafin said about the reflections on the canals was right.

Poor Serafin. What had become of him?

'Look ahead!' cried Vermithrax. 'Look left and to the south!'

They had all three known that a moment would come when they faced the Pharaoh's fighting forces. But so much had happened since they left the Campanile. The terrors of the encircling besiegers had come to seem vague and distant to Merle.

Now, however, the time was here. In a few minutes they would be flying over the circle. It was still just a blurred line on the horizon, but it was coming closer and closer.

'I shall have to climb very high,' Vermithrax said. 'The air will be thinner up there, so don't be afraid if you find breathing a little difficult.'

'I won't.' Merle tried to make her voice sound firm.

The lion's huge obsidian wings carried them up and up, until the sea below became a regular, flat surface without waves or currents.

Far ahead, Merle saw the Pharaoh's war galleys, tiny as toys. The distance did not deceive her: those ships had destructive power enough to crush the inadequate Venetian fleet within hours. The same ships had spread the first plagues of scarab beetles all over the world at the very beginning of the Great War of the Mummies. Those little eating machines, no bigger than a human thumb but compounded of chitin and malice, had rolled inexorably over the world's continents. First crops, then livestock, and finally human beings had fallen victim to them. And the armies of mummies had followed the scarabs in their thousands of thousands, torn from their graves by Pharaoh's high priests, armed and sent into battle, with no will of their own and unable to feel pain.

The Great War had lasted thirteen years, and then its outcome was decided – as if there had ever been any doubt about it. The Egyptian Empire had enslaved the other nations, and its armies marched along the roads of the entire globe.

Merle crouched lower on the stone lion's mane, as if that could save her from the danger threatening from the surface of the sea below.

The hulls of the galleys were painted gold, for the indestructible skin of the Egyptian desert gods was golden too. Each galley had three masts and many sails. Two rows of long oars emerged from the sides of the hulls. And the prow of every ship had a tall superstructure, with an altar on which the high priests in their golden robes offered sacrifices – usually of animals, though many people spoke darkly of human sacrifice as well.

Small steamers cruised among the galleys. Their tasks were reconnaissance, supply and pursuit. The besieging ring was about five hundred metres broad, stretching over the sea both ways until it reached the coasts, where it was continued on land by various formations of war machines and infantrymen, thousands upon thousands of mummy warriors who had no will of their own, but awaited the signal to attack. It was only a question of days now before the final confirmation reached the Pharaoh's commanders: without the Flowing Queen, Venice was defenceless and ready to fall.

Merle closed her eyes in despair, but the voice of Vermithrax brought her back from her thoughts again. 'Are those the flying ships you spoke of?' He sounded both baffled and fascinated.

'Barques of the Sun,' Merle confirmed, her voice strained as she looked ahead over his flying mane. 'Do you think they've seen us?'

'It doesn't look like it.'

Half a dozen slender shapes were cruising at some distance from them. Vermithrax was flying higher than the aircraft; with a little luck they would pass unobserved by the captains of the barques.

The Empire's Barques of the Sun gleamed golden, like the galleys, and as they were closer to the sky than the mighty battleships down on the sea, the glitter of their hulls was much brighter. They were three times as long as a Venetian gondola, roofed over, and with narrow, horizontal window slits in their sides. From outside, it was impossible to see how many men they carried behind those windows. Merle estimated that a barque would have room for ten people at most: a captain, eight crew members, and the priest whose magic kept them airborne. In sunlight, the slender airships could manoeuvre very fast and were as light as a feather. If the sky was cloudy, their speed slowed down and their movements were clumsy. It was almost impossible to fly them by night.

Now, however, the bright morning sun was shining in the sky. The barques glittered like the eyes of beasts of prey against a blurred background of land and water.

'We'll be above them any moment,' said Vermithrax.

Merle was breathing more quickly. The obsidian lion had been right: the air was thin up here and hurt her chest. But she did not say so out loud; she was simply thankful that Vermithrax was strong enough to carry her so high, up and away over the Egyptians.

'*We've nearly made it*,' said the Flowing Queen. Her voice sounded strained.

The Barques of the Sun were directly below them now, like shining sword blades hovering around the lagoon, describing wide arcs as they flew. No one on board would be expecting to see a solitary lion in flight. The attention of the captains was turned on the city, not on the air above their heads.

Vermithrax lost height again. Gratefully, Merle felt her lungs fill with air more quickly. But her spellbound gaze was still turned on the barques, now retreating ever faster behind them.

'Can we be seen from the galleys?' she asked hoarsely.

No one answered her.

'*We've done it!*' exulted the Flowing Queen.

'It would have been odd if we hadn't,' growled Vermithrax.

Only Merle remained unmoved. And only after a while did she speak up again. 'Didn't you notice anything?'

'What do you mean?' asked the lion.

'It was so quiet.'

'We were flying too high to hear anything,' said Vermithrax. 'Sounds don't reach so far.'

'*Yes, they do,*' the Queen contradicted Vermithrax, although he could not hear her. '*You're right, Merle. There's complete silence on the galleys. A deathly silence.*'

'You mean –'

'*Mummy warriors. Those ships are manned by living corpses. Like almost all the Empire's war machines. The graveyards of the countries they conquered give the priests an inexhaustible supply of reinforcements. The only living men on board are the high priests themselves and the ships' captains.*'

Merle lapsed into a deep silence. The idea of all those dead people fighting for the Pharaoh terrified her as much as the thought of what still lay ahead of them.

'Where are we flying to?' she asked a little later. They had flown around the Pharaoh's army in a wide curve and were moving inland at last.

'I would like to see my home again,' growled Vermithrax.

'No!' said the Flowing Queen, and for the first time she used Merle's voice to speak aloud. 'Ours is another destination, Vermithrax.'

'The lion's wings beat irregularly for a moment. 'Queen?' he asked uncertainly. 'Is that you?'

Merle tried to say something, but to her horror the Flowing Queen's will imposed itself on her own, suppressing her words. She realised, with crystal clarity, that from now on her body was not hers alone.

'Yes, Vermithrax, I am here. It's been a long time.'

'Indeed, Queen.'

'Will you help me?'

The lion hesitated, and then nodded his mighty, obsidian head. 'I will.'

'Then listen to what I have to say. You too, Merle. My plan involves us all.'

And then words entirely unknown to Merle passed her lips: places and ideas, and over and over again a single name.

Lord Light.

She had no idea what this was all about, and she wasn't even sure that she wanted to know more just now. For the moment, nothing could disturb or shake her. They had broken through the encircling ring of besiegers, that was what counted. They had escaped the clutches of the biggest army the world had ever seen. Merle's relief was so overwhelming that all the Flowing Queen's plans and gloomy prophecies bounced off her as if they had nothing to do with herself.

Her heart was racing as if to burst her ribcage, the blood was rushing in her ears, her eyes burned with the wind blowing into them. Never mind. They had escaped.

She looked back several times and saw the rows of galleys and the fleets of the Barques of the Sun dwindle and finally disappear entirely in the blurred blue and grey of the horizon. Only grains of sand, in a world too mighty to stand by any longer and put up with all the wrongs done to it by the Egyptians.

Something was going to happen, Merle suddenly knew it. Something great, fantastic. As if in a lighting flash, she realised that this was indeed only the beginning. Child's play by comparison with what lay ahead of them.

And gradually it dawned on her that fate had given her a special part to play in all of this. Her, and the Flowing Queen, and perhaps Vermithrax too.

Although the Queen was still speaking through her,

although her lips kept moving as they formed the strange words, Merle allowed herself the luxury of closing her eyes. A little rest. At last. She just wanted to be alone with herself for a moment. It was almost surprising to find that she could do it, in spite of the guest she carried within her.

Then they reached the mainland and were flying over drought-ridden fields, bare mountainsides, charred villages, and for a long, long time none of them said a word.

Lord Light. The words echoed in Merle's mind. She hoped they would provoke the voice inside into some reaction, into giving some kind of explanation.

But the Flowing Queen kept silent.

Merle's fingers burrowed deeper into the lion's obsidian mane. Something to hold on to. A good feeling among so many bad ones.

In the distance she saw mountain peaks far, far away on the horizon. The land stretching all the way from the sea to those mountains had once been full of human beings, full of life.

But now nothing lived here. No plants, no animals, no human beings – nothing.

'*They are all dead*,' said the Flowing Queen quietly.

Merle felt the change that came over Vermithrax even

before she stretched out her hand and felt something wet.

She realised that the obsidian lion was weeping.

'*All dead*,' whispered the Queen.

And after that they said no more, but looked towards the distant mountain range.